The Pagoda in the Garden

The
Pagoda *in*
the Garden

A NOVEL IN THREE PARTS

Wendy Lesser

HANDSEL BOOKS

an imprint of
Other Press • New York

Production Editor: Robert D. Hack

This book was set in Centaur MT by Alpha Graphics of Pittsfield, NH.

10 9 8 7 6 5 4 3 2 1

Library of Congress Cataloging-in-Publication Data
Lesser, Wendy.
   The pagoda in the garden / by Wendy Lesser.
      p. cm.
   ISBN 1-59051-176-X
   1. Americans—Europe—Fiction. 2. Authors—Fiction.
3. England—Fiction. 4. Europe—Fiction. I. Title.
   PS3612.E8186P34 2005
   813'.6—dc22
                                                    2004027427

For Arthur Lubow,
and in memory of Thom Gunn

Contents

Book One: 1901/1926   1

Book Two: 1956   87

Book Three: 1973–1975   125

Book One
1901/1926

THE INVITATION SAT propped between the silver triangles of the toast rack. One of the charms of this small, well-run hotel—one of the charms of London, she always reminded herself—was that one could get breakfast and the day's first post at the same time. Not that the invitation had arrived precisely *in* the toast rack: that degree of levity would have struck the management as unseemly. No, she had set it there herself, after reading it once; and now, as she thoughtfully eyed it from a distance, over her second cup of morning coffee (a French habit that had become impossible to break), she seemed to ask of it a degree of communication that went beyond the mere explicitness of black scrawl on cream pasteboard.

It was silent, however, on the subject that for the moment preoccupied her, which was how best to present its contents to Gilbert. Roderick had not, of course, issued the invitation to them jointly, but there would be no difficulty, she knew, in procuring an additional, separate card for Gilbert if that proved necessary. Or desirable—for she was not at all sure she wanted Gilbert leaning over her shoulder, as it were, vicariously perusing every passage of her social existence. It was not that he would fail to take the meaning of the occasion in its proper manner (that is, according to her own, their own, very singular lights); nor that he would fall in any way short of what might be expected of him, individually or socially, by her or by anyone else. On the contrary, he was nothing if not unremittingly correct and tactful, at least in the public sphere. That, perhaps, was the problem with him: he was "nothing" when not precisely that, and the unremittingness of it was beginning to strike her as sorely trying her capacity for credit.

This was not a new realization. She'd been round it several times already, circling and sniffing like a spoiled lapdog faced with a morsel that needed at some point to be eaten but couldn't at present quite be stomached. She would have been happier, under the posited circumstances, not to have any sense of smell at all, to be able to gobble up what nourished her without the resistances and questionings that never seemed, as far as she could tell, to trouble other people to anything like the same degree. But spoiled she was—though, granted, she'd done it to herself, through the years of following her own wishes, discriminating among her own possible choices, ignoring the insistences and regimentations of both family and convention. And now it was left to her to reap the disadvantages of being spoiled in that way. The money had, of course, contributed, but it had not by any means been the whole story; for she knew, with a certainty transcending all empirical evidence, that had she been born a New York washerwoman's daughter, she would nonetheless (if she had managed to survive her childhood) now be sniffing round her fate with exactly the same degree of hesitation that presently informed her every consideration.

Her every *move*, she had almost thought, and then thought better, for it was precisely in the area of motion that she was most decisive. If she had not been astute enough to perceive this about herself, others would in any case have pointed it out to her. Roderick himself called her the Whirling Dervish (W.D., in affectionate shorthand), frequently pointing out that it never took him less than three weeks to recuperate from the exhaustion of one day spent with her. This, at least, was true of the days they spent in London, which is why he was now suggesting she come for a midweek stay at Grantchester, where the flat stillness of the surrounding landscape and the quiet amenities of his Shepard House would contrive to keep down the level of her habitual nervous excitement. Even the presence of a small house party—even, he added, the relative proximity of the great and bustling University—wouldn't, by comparison, set off the extravagant expenditures of energy that characterized her London life.

She agreed, and further agreed with what was unsaid (and remained unknown, to him): that she needed a few days away from Gilbert to recover her spirits, or her self-possession, or whatever it was the young man so innocently robbed her of. For innocent he always was; therein lay both the depth and the shallowness of his capacity to harm. No hurt rendered by him was ever intentional—not so much because he was incapable of ill will (though he probably was, she conceded) as because he was incapable of *anything* she herself would describe as will, or intention, or considered action. He was pure intuition, pure responsiveness, pure spontaneous life. It was this, of course, which had initially attracted her to him, and this which now caused her to think of him as so curiously but still alluringly "empty." His was not the emptiness of stupidity—he was always quick enough off the mark, in conversation or anything else, once she had set the tone and the direction. No, it was a deeper and more frightening kind of emptiness than that, as if he had no desires other than the ones he perceived she wanted him to have. If she'd been able to conceive of herself as a religious woman, she'd have described him as having no soul.

The innocent young devil made his appearance at that moment, as if, Faustlike, she had called him up. But he, more prosaic than Mephistopheles, came through a door: the door, to be exact, which separated their adjoining suites. Part of what she treasured about her London hotel—part of what made it, on her extended stays in this country, *their* London hotel—was the management's ability to keep up all the comforts and appearances of utter respectability while simultaneously catering to her less respectable desires. ("Respectable" according to whose lights—her own or the world's—was a question she had not yet answered for herself, in large measure because she refused even to ask it.) This matter of the communicating rooms was something which by now had become so usual as to be, in their detailed preliminary arrangements, entirely unspoken.

As he came into the room, he paused for a moment to glance at the headlines of the day's *Times*, a copy of which had courteously been left on the table for her eventual perusal.

"How is she?"

" 'She'?" He appeared genuinely confused.

"The Queen, of course."

"Oh, yes." He glanced again. "Not well, they say. Worsening, I would guess, though they're too diplomatic to say so.

But why are you so concerned? She isn't even your Queen, after all."

"Why not? An American girl can grow up thinking about princesses too, you know. And she has been the Queen for my entire life. It's been one of the few permanencies. I can't explain exactly why, but my whole sense of who I am is tied to her. When she dies, I will realize for the first time that I too am growing old."

"Hardly old!" He laughed, then saw she was quite serious. Striding quickly over to her, he caressed her cheek with the palm of his hand. "To me you will always seem an adventurous little girl."

"Patently false, but I thank you for saying it." She covered his hand for a moment with hers, then let it go. "At any rate, there's a more practical concern. I gather I'm to be invited to the State Funeral. She was—she *is*—apparently one of the numerous throng of admiring readers. Of course, nothing's been said explicitly in advance; that would be unbearably crude and morbid. But there have been hints."

"How jolly for you!"

"To reap publicity from a beloved monarch's death? Ghoulish, I'd say."

"Oh, Charlotte, you know what I mean. You deserve the attention as well as anyone. Try not to pretend otherwise."

They were both silent at this—she at receiving, he at having administered the tender rebuke. She broke the silence with a change of subject.

"Look," she said, handing him the card and deciding in that gestural moment what her tack was to be. "Roderick wants me to come down next week. Do you think I ought to go?"

It was the "ought," she knew, which would determine his response. The implication of a social obligation, combined with the slightest hint of her desire to resist such a duty, would be enough. For he knew that in their dealings with each other, private as well as public, it was his role to urge the importance of convention whenever she expressed a wish to abrogate it.

He took the bit of closely scribbled pasteboard from her and, reading it quickly, handed it back with a smile. Roderick's habitual approach to her—both his exaggerated conception of her dauntlessness and his wittily allusive means of formulating that exaggeration—never failed to produce this reaction. It was as if Gilbert couldn't quite see the truth of the conception himself but nevertheless found it funny, attributing the humor entirely to Roderick's own peculiar way of seeing things.

"Yes, of course you should," he said. "The old boy will be immensely disappointed if you don't."

"Shall I get him to invite you as well?" To an observer, it might have seemed as if something hung fire between them; but she knew, even if he didn't (and of that she could never be sure), that the conclusion was already foregone.

"No, no." He waved away the very idea with a flick of his hand. "I'll be fine here for a few days. London is filled with entertainments of one sort or another at this time of year, and if I feel unbearably solitary I can always look up some of the fellows at the club."

Though she was expecting and indeed planning on the refusal, it still gave her a small pang. Was this because he showed himself so capable of doing without her for a few days? Or was it simply the predictability, the calculable procurability, of his response? Or (and here she began to feel herself coming closer to the mark) did the exactness of his plans, the length and detail of his polite refusal, suggest to her that in fact there was some entirely other possibility, unmentioned in his list, that could serve to occupy his time? However empty a vessel she considered him to be, she nonetheless didn't like to feel that someone else might be using him for storage during her absence.

She didn't, at any rate, reply to his demurral, but instead looked down again at the invitation he'd returned to her. A flicker of amusement crossed her face, and he caught it in an instant.

"I liked that bit about the date," he chimed in, striking the exact note that had already been ringing in her own mind. "How does he put it? 'The first house party of the new century, if we align ourselves with the mathematicians rather than the journalists.' Typical of Roderick Stephen to be a year late on everything, and consider it fashionable to be so."

"It's an old joke of ours," she explained. "Last year he wrote me a letter that began in late 1899 and finished in early 1900, and he made in passing some kind of joke about having held the letter over 'to the next century—if next century it be.' He took a very superior tone to those who cared desperately whether the new century began in 1900 or 1901. So of course I mocked him for his vaunted superiority, to time as well as to society, and we've had a running joke about it ever since." She smiled up at him, as if having explained all.

He took the smile as a sort of invitation, and dropped gracefully into the chaise next to her chair, which brought a different angle to his gaze and converted her, for the moment, into the superior party. But however lowered its point of origin, his glance at her was no less direct than before; if any-thing, it sharpened.

"Do you think he's in love with you?" he asked. His hand-some eyes narrowed, whether with amusement or concern she couldn't be sure. Then his sweetly expressive lips parted in a slight smile, as if to sway the balance toward humor.

She, however, was not to be swayed. "Don't be silly," she almost snapped. She blushed, and then blushed more intensely as he appeared to take note of her revealing complexion. "You know his interests don't lie in that direction."

"Oh, yes, I've heard all about that. But I don't think the two are mutually exclusive. Do you?"

She felt him putting more than the usual emphasis on that last interrogation. It amused but also gratified her to think that he too was capable of jealousy, especially in regard to such an unlikely object.

"Not in everyone," she said. "But in Roderick's case it's more than he can do to sustain such a fascination with one person, one type, beyond himself. Not himself, exactly—it's not his own person that so absorbs his passion, but his work, which he sees as something quite outside himself." She paused a moment. "So you see your little theory is quite wrong."

"Ah," he said, as he rose to leave her to her morning's work, "then perhaps it's you who are in love with him."

THAT'S AS FAR as I got when I tried to tell the story— whenever it was, in 1902 or 1903, shortly after it was all over and I'd gone back to France. It was a good story. I still think it was a good story. But it was a story that couldn't be told properly in the language of that time, at least in my language at that time, which took its cue so strongly from Roderick's own. He was such a powerful presence. I don't think anyone who wasn't alive then, who wasn't a fully conscious adult then, can sense what it was like to be writing at the same time he was. It was simply impossible, if you admired him at all, to strike out on your own separate path. It was as if he took up all the available oxygen in the literary universe—breathed it in through those long, sinuous, subtly inflected sentences of his, and only doled out his exhalations to the rest of us.

But I'm not being entirely fair, or truthful. And if I'm to render him, if I'm to render *us*, as anything like what we really were, then fairness or truthfulness or something combining them must be my keynote. It's all I have left of him, all he gave me that's still useful now. Perhaps the word I'm search- ing for is integrity. In my notes to myself, I once wrote about Roderick (that wasn't his real name, of course, but I'll keep it here—you know his real name): "Roderick has more integ- rity than anyone I know. Maybe more integrity than is good for him—more integrity than tact, more integrity than loyalty, certainly more integrity than mercy, possibly more integrity than love (though he would say that love from someone without integrity isn't worth anything)."

I'm losing my thread. I was going to say something about the difficulty—that it wasn't just a linguistic difficulty, not just a matter of getting free of his pondering, evasive, monumental language. It was also a matter of things we didn't say then. You have no idea how much the world has changed in just twenty-five years. At my age, a quarter of a century seems like nothing, a few years back in my adult memory. But the whole world has altered unrecognizably since then, in ways we had no possibility of foreseeing. I don't just mean the War, though that was a tremendous shock, an absolute disillusionment. But everything else too. Everything that's part of what you take for granted: automobiles and moving pictures, radio waves and electric power, newspaper empires and American big business—and Americans all over the world, everybody having now become an American—and people flying miles above the earth, and digging miles into it, nothing left intact or inaccessible. You can't imagine how that alters the way one looks at things.

Well, I'm supposed to be sitting here writing a speech, and indeed I am. Such generalizations. Roderick would be ashamed of me. But he would agree—would be forced to agree, painfully—that the world he knew, and that I knew with him, is truly gone.

Still, it's not all bad. Some of the younger men, and the women too, have done wonderful things with the new world, the new language. That fiery young man who writes about sex and power and madness and civilization—they say he's the one who should be getting the prize instead of me. They say he *would* be getting the prize instead of me, if the government hadn't stepped in and forbidden it. Un-American, I think they called his work. A strange term. I'm sorry if they think mine's American; I never meant it to be.

But I'm not getting anywhere with the speech. You would think this lovely view of the park and the beautifully fitted-out desk and the comfortable hotel room would all be conducive to it. And the weather. It's too cold to go outside, even for a quick walk around the lake. So I have all these hours, hours amounting to days, to spend alone at my desk. No one I know lives in New York anymore. I wonder who will come to the ceremony? No one *I* know, except some of those faded old has-beens whom I've always avoided, and who now declare themselves to be the authorities, the prize-givers. Ah, well, I shouldn't complain. They're giving it to me. I really *must* get this acceptance speech written before the ceremony. But I just can't keep my mind on the speech. When I pick up my pen, all I can think about is that unfinished novel, and the lost world it belonged to.

HE, MEANWHILE, HAD been thrown into a state which in any less substantial person might have been described as a tizzy. The same morning's mail which had brought Charlotte his invitation had delivered to Roderick a letter from Rome.

Sifting desultorily through the envelopes that Pierce had placed, as usual, on the sideboard in the front hallway, he felt his pulse quicken at the sight of the familiar handwriting on the lightweight foreign stationery. He admonished himself immediately—pulse-quickening was for younger, thinner, more hopeful characters—and then gave up the admonition. Who was he to deplore any signs of hopefulness and youthful romanticism, even in his staid old self? Especially in his staid old self, he felt called upon to add, since it was in regard to the motions of his own heart (or mind, or whatever produced such flutters) that he found himself least able either to deplore or to command with anything resembling rational conviction.

Conviction, rational or otherwise, had at any rate little to do with his relation to Antonio. In fact, he wondered to himself, on this particular morning as on so many other occasions, whether he had ever been as unconvinced of anything as he was of Antonio. It was not only the young man's self-announced artistic talent that struck him as lacking in complete credibility. Nor was the feeling of insubstantiality produced entirely by his curious sense, whenever Antonio was at a distance (or even momentarily out of the room), that he had simply made the creature up wholesale. That phantasmal quality, after all, was very evidently part of the young sculptor's charm for him. No, what left him in greatest doubt was the absolute unanswerability of the question he repeatedly asked himself, the question as to his own deepest, darkest motives in allowing and even encouraging the friendship. What, finally, did he hope to "get" out of it? Or, if that verb implied too fiduciary a transaction, sounded too much of the ever-clamoring din of the marketplace, then where, in more gentle terms, did he hope to find himself at the end of it? What could he possibly imagine *as* the end of it? And what, finally, did he mean by "it"?

That there was something between them, at least on his own side, was amply suggested by the deplorable (if only briefly deplored) flutter of his pulse. That Antonio too had a stake in these matters, whatever "these matters" might eventually prove to be, was suggested no less by the contents of his letter. He proposed a visit, a visit so imminent as to be unpreventable, since he would already have left his Rome address by the time his note arrived at "tu bella casa," as he so inappropriately (because so un-Englishly) described Shepard House. It was no accident that all of Roderick's prior meetings with Antonio had taken place on the latter's native ground, for it was only there that the older man could summon up even a modicum of the required belief in the younger one's seriousness, not to mention existence. An Antonio in England would be a flight of fancy so outlandish, so unimaginable, that Roderick had never before even remotely entertained it. Yet the unimaginable was about to descend on him—was about to do so, moreover, in precisely the week for which he had invited Charlotte.

The others could, if necessary, be put off; they lived in the immediate neighborhood, and it was possible that Pierce had not yet even dispatched the cards inviting them. But Charlotte would by now have received the note, would be planning— if indeed she were able to come at all—to make an entire jaunt of it. Charlotte was not a woman with whose schedule he felt anxious to trifle, and to send at this point a second note withdrawing the warmly issued invitation would certainly smack of trifling. As he reflected further on it, the thought came to Roderick that Charlotte's presence on those particular days would not be an undesirable thing. She, after all, knew Antonio; knew, furthermore, *about* Antonio in more detail than any of Roderick's other English friends (if that nationality could, in an honorary sense, be conferred on an American woman who spent most of her time in France). She had ways of being helpful in touchy situations, of drawing people out or keeping them in as the circumstances required. She was, in short, a "managing" woman in all the best (and a few of the worst) senses of the word. With her here, he might even venture to restore a few other members of the house party— not for the week, perhaps, but for a day. Yes, it would possibly work out: Charlotte and Antonio as the intimate circle in residence, and three or four others for, say, Tuesday afternoon and evening. Mrs. Pierce could then exert herself entirely on the single dinner party, leaving the two guests and their host to get by as best they could on the remaining days.

It occurred to Roderick that he had not actually set eyes on Mrs. Pierce for quite some time now. But this did not concern him. Often the excesses of the holiday season, exacerbated by the celebrations of the New Year, had a withering effect on her, at least for a week or so. It was with this in mind that he had set the house party for later in the month, just past its midpoint—to give her, as it were, a chance to gird up her loins. In the meantime he had become quite adept, with Pierce's assistance, at "fending for himself" (as he characterized the recklessly provisional nature of his current domestic existence, on the infrequent occasions when he bothered to characterize it at all). At any rate, meals of some sort continuing to emerge from the kitchen at regular intervals, he neither knew nor cared how this was accomplished, as long as they routinely arrived at the moments when he habitually chose to set down his pen.

It was, as this thought now reminded him, time again to take up that pen. He had already wasted too many precious minutes on the anxieties induced by Antonio's letter; and the prospect of Charlotte's clarifying presence and assistance would serve, for the moment, as a beacon to keep off further darkness. In the meantime, *Harper's* was clamoring for the next installment, and he was more than uncomfortably aware of the need to generate sufficient material to feed that growling beast. His discomfort was, in this case, greater than usual, not only because he was in danger of exceeding the contractual length by many thousands of words (*that*, at any rate, he had done before), but because this new tale was something of a departure from his usual mode. The contract had been signed, however, and serial publication was about to begin, so however much his employers disliked what he gave them, it was unlikely that they would have the nerve to staunch the flow of words in midstream, no matter how far out to sea his uncharted voyaging might eventually take him.

THERE, YOU SEE, I find it impossible to imagine Roderick in anything but his own language. I did try. I thought, with all these years gone by, that I could begin to see him differently, from the outside, from modernity's perspective. But he creates his own version of "modernity," insists on it, speaks it into existence. And he imposes it on the whole world around him, so that the rest of us become merely his creatures, his characters. I know I should be able to get free of him—I have, after all, survived him. That should count for something. But it doesn't seem to matter. He takes over my pen (not such a very different pen from the one he was using to compose that "new tale" in 1901—we old folks do stick to our habits). He refuses to acknowledge that *I'm* the survivor, and instead tries to outlive me, through me. Ah, well, I'll probably let him have his way; I always did.

THE LAST TEN minutes of a train journey were, for Charlotte, always the hardest. Her destination having been announced, she would put away her book or periodical and ready herself for arrival. But, Charlotte being what she was, her readiness always came far in advance of the train's, and she was left to stare out the window at the often-too-familiar landscape— for most of her journeys, at this point, were to places she had already been, life's daily adventurousness proving, in middle age, to make the geographical explorations of her earlier years unnecessary. She had heard praises from more sources than she cared to recall (most of them, she reminded herself, insularly British) of the English countryside. But even the most enthusiastic of these nature-worshippers had little to say in favor of the nondescript fenland surrounding Cambridge. If rural landscape at its best rarely interested Charlotte, she could hardly fail to be bored at what she now saw passing by her train window.

The train did, however, finally pull into Cambridge station, a garish brick structure which she had always considered more suited to the smoky ambitions of a factory town than the contemplative ones of a great university. And there was Roderick's country cart awaiting her, complete with the gentleman-farmer himself at its reins.

"Well, Roderick," she called as she emerged from the station, ignoring the efforts of the attendant to help her with her single small valise, "I see you haven't left off the agricultural affectations yet."

"Come, my dear W.D., what do you expect me to do? Hire a London hansom cab for your arrival?"

She smiled. "That would be excessive, and you are never that. But a horse-and-cart almost errs in the other direction—so defiantly rural. And you know how I *despise* everything connected with the country." Her comic emphasis softened the remark, even as it hinted at a core of truth.

"I do know, and am all the more flattered that you didn't let this curious disability prevent you from visiting me."

He had by this time lifted her bag into the back of the cart and handed his guest herself onto the cushion beside him. Glancing quickly but affectionately at his large, stern, familiar face, she gave his hand a warm squeeze before releasing it.

It had often puzzled her, this sense she had of caring more for Roderick—for his good opinion, of course, but also for his person—than anyone else in the world. It was not that she lacked other attachments; attachments (especially if Roderick's view of her was to be believed) were what she had altogether too many of. Nor was it that she and Roderick confided deeply in each other. In merely conversational terms, she exchanged much more with Gilbert, or even with half-a-dozen more casual friends. But perhaps it was precisely in this absence of conversational probing that her intimacy with Roderick lay. They knew each other without having to know the details; they communed silently. And if this silence served to perpetuate certain illusions he might have about her virginal devotion to their craft—well, so much the better. In the privacy of her own mind she might acknowledge herself to be sentimentally dependent—to need the prop of a sexual liaison, and not merely desire it—but in Roderick's company she could temporarily feel herself to have been released from all such longings. As long as he believed she breathed the same high, pure air that he did, she could almost come to believe it herself. This, she assured herself, and no more conventional reason, was why she kept hidden from him the nature of her relationship with Gilbert. It was true that he might not be shocked (and Gilbert, for one, repeatedly insisted he would not). But in the absence of his shock she might discover something she did not wish to know. If Roderick presumed her, as a matter of course, to be sullied with the trappings of mundane needs and affections—if he presumed her, in that respect, to be different from himself—she wanted to remain forever ignorant of that fact. Indeed, an external observer of her situation might have noted a singular irony: she had thus far been so successful in remaining ignorant that she was not even aware of the wish to do so.

Turning slightly in his seat to address her, as he jauntily slapped the cart-horse's back with the reins, Roderick asked, apropos of nothing, "And how's that interesting mutual friend of ours, the fair Gilbert?"

It was not the first time he had seemed to read her thoughts. Yet Charlotte knew that his penetrating vision was in many ways a parlor trick, a game that he won so often only because others routinely assumed he had been dealt a winning hand. He had a reputation for psychological perceptiveness, and therefore his interlocutors confessed everything to him, marveling afterward that he had been able to see through them so well. She, however, was not to be taken in that easily; she knew a coincidence from an intention, and could act accordingly.

"He is as fair as ever," she responded blithely, "and sends you his regards. I saw him at one of the Duchess's evenings just before I left London, and when he learned I was coming here he became effusive in his praises of you, evidently meaning them to be conveyed. But why do you call him 'interesting' when he's never produced anything in his life?"

"That in itself shows his excellent aesthetic sensibility. To know when not to 'produce,' as you call it, is as valuable as knowing when to do so—and much rarer."

"Well, I'm glad one of us has faith in Gilbert's sensibility."

"It's you who should believe in his taste, dear, since I'm convinced he worships you. At a respectful distance, of course."

"Of course." She gave him a sharp look, but he responded only with a bland, reassuring smile.

"Speaking of respectful distances, we are to have an unexpected visitor from afar this week." He stopped, as if this alone should have been sufficient to tell her the identity of the mysterious guest; but when her raised eyebrows indicated her still-unfulfilled curiosity, he went on. "From Rome." He dropped it as a terminally conclusive hint.

"Not—?"

"I'm afraid so."

Charlotte knew that his phrase contained elements of both the conventional and the true—both the convention of a host's regret at anything unexpected, and the actual fear that Antonio's presence in England would be bound to arouse in him. She thought she knew, moreover, precisely the degree to which this fear stemmed from his own emotional uncertainties and warinesses, and not from the potential responses (whether condemnatory or congratulatory) that might be aroused in observers. However concerned he was with appearances, he was finally not one to place great weight in the opinions of others. The problem, for him, would be to determine exactly what his own opinions were.

Whatever Roderick's views about Antonio's visit might cautiously and belatedly be, Charlotte's own reaction was instantaneous if complex. Her self-confessed curiosity at the opportunity of seeing Antonio under Roderick's roof was more than outweighed, at least in this initial moment, by the jealous knowledge that she was not, after all, to be the most favored guest. She had left behind Gilbert; was it not fair to expect some equivalent sacrifice from him?

Charlotte mentally castigated herself for the unjustness of her thought. Roderick would emphasize—*had* emphasized, in their lengthy conversation and correspondence over the years—just how far from equivalent their situations were. "It's not just the relative impropriety," he had said, "for I grant that an unmarried woman can be unfairly accused of impropriety as well. It's not, for that matter, to do with any social condition at all—even (if I can call this a 'social' condition) with your being a woman and my being a man. It has, on the contrary, everything (or as close to everything as makes no difference) to do with our individual natures. For you, it's always possible, in personal relations, to do exactly what you want, to take things only as far as seems sensible, and to eliminate or ignore or in some other way exclude the elements that might create difficulties."

She could not help but feel, at this point, that he underrated the unmanageability of her desires, but since she wanted him to have no detailed knowledge either of the desires or their unmanageability, she let this pass.

"Whereas in my case," he had continued, "I can only, I fear, want what I don't have and shun what's readily available to me. With me, it's not a matter of renunciation, or anything as high-flown as that; if it were, perhaps I could at least claim some moral credit. No, if I renounce, it's solely in order to ensure that the object retains its desirability for me."

She turned toward him, now, a face that reflected, insofar as she could control her expression, only the acceptable portion of the curiosity and none of the resentment that she had just discerned in herself. "It will be interesting to see Antonio in England."

"Interesting? Ah, if I had some assurance that it would be only that!"

She needn't, as it turned out, have worried quite so much about being displaced from the position of honor, for Antonio didn't appear at the scheduled time. She had only been in the house an hour or two when the telegram arrived announcing his delay (an announcement that, typically, referred only to the delay itself and gave neither a reason nor a new time of arrival). That couple of hours had, however, been sufficient for her to discover that Shepard House was not at its most accommodating. From the mudstained front hallway to the cold upper reaches, the entire house carried a dank, mildewish smell. A heavy layer of dust covered much of the dark woodwork, made darker not only by the wintry light but by the near-total absence of oil in the old lamps set about the house. The pale glow cast by the few gas fixtures was sufficient, however, to convey the extent of the chaos. In fact, Charlotte felt she had rarely seen Shepard House in such a state of dirt and disorder, though Roderick himself appeared not to notice.

"Where are the Pierces?" she asked him, poking her head into the study, where he had resumed his work after showing her the telegram. "I was hoping to get some fresh linen for my bath, but no one responded to the bell."

"Oh, my dear!" He got up with an expression of intense if rather misdirected concern. "How perfectly awful. I must have given them the afternoon off without thinking about it. I suppose I assumed you'd bring your own maid with you."

"My own maid wanted to visit her sister's family in Hackney, and since I was to be away this week I thought it would be the opportune moment to let her go. But sit down, sit down—there's nothing to get excited about. I'll telegraph her this evening, and she'll be here by tomorrow. I suppose Pierce can at least take a telegram to town for me? They *will* get back, I assume, by teatime?"

"Well, perhaps not by teatime—I often just boil up a cup for myself. But surely by dinner. In any case, what shall we do about your linen? I could get you a bath-towel and flannel from my own dressing-room—"

"Sit down, Roderick. I'm perfectly capable of finding my own towels, thank you, and I wouldn't even have mentioned it if it hadn't seemed odd. I think I remember vaguely where Mrs. Pierce's linen cupboard is."

"Good, good," he mumbled, immersed again in his writing before she had even quietly closed the door. It was such a comfort, he observed to himself, to have a houseguest competent enough to take care of herself.

Charlotte, in search of the airing cupboard, idly recalled the eccentricities of character Mrs. Pierce had displayed on her previous visits. They were evidently, for Roderick, part of the background atmosphere of Shepard House; like the present confusion, they were something he simply didn't notice. Charlotte was not surprised to find that things had deteriorated this far without his making any effort to reverse the decline. "Well, my good woman," she addressed the absent Mrs. Pierce, "you'll soon shape up under *my* supervision."

Her tone sharpened considerably when she discovered the linen cupboard to be empty. How could a household be entirely bereft of clean towels? It had never happened before in Charlotte's experience; it had never before been known to happen during a house party. She shook her head at Roderick's evident laxity, and then went in search of the towels he had offered her before, from his own dressing room. These ones, she observed, were somewhat the worse for wear, and she hesitated a moment before taking one. But Charlotte was a practical woman, and prided herself on not being finicky; so she sniffed among the available choices and took the bath-towel that gave off the least aroma, exclaiming inwardly that Mrs. Pierce was going to have a great deal to answer for.

I KNOW WE don't talk about servants like that any more. We don't, in general, even *have* servants—at least, I haven't had any since the War, barring the daily people like the housekeeper and the gardener, who come in from outside. We don't live with them any more. Maybe a more accurate way of putting it is that they won't live with us.

Still, I don't see why I should feel embarrassed about Charlotte's opinions. She's not I, after all. And I don't mean that in any coy sense. It's not just that twenty-five years— those twenty-five years that have made us all so unrecognizable—have passed since then. Nor is it the mere convention of pronouns, that transformation from first to third which makes everything so much more placeable, and in which Henry Adams is our acknowledged national master. No, I really mean that she doesn't represent me accurately. She keeps thinking things I wouldn't think, saying things I never said, even doing things I couldn't possibly do. Oh, I'm not denying there's a skeleton of truth hidden inside this story—but it's only the skeleton. Everything *you* see, everything on the outside, is made up, or at least transformed. I am no more Charlotte than he is Roderick.

But I do feel constricted by Charlotte's viewpoint. I long to tear open that suffocatingly self-analyzing prison and escape into something clearer, something less nuanced and attenuated. Let us have some fact for a change, some incident. Let us really see Shepard House and its inhabitants from the outside. "There is no 'outside,'" Roderick was always insisting. "Everything must be transmitted through an individual sensibility—as it is in life." But even he broke his own rules sometimes.

Actually, I'm beginning to dig my way out, if ever so slowly. Did you catch the detail about the smelly towels? Roderick would never have mentioned such a thing. I don't believe there's a single reference to bed or bath linen in his entire *oeuvre*; certainly not dirty linen. That's a touch I must have picked up from the new generation, the brutal natural-ists, like the young man who should be getting my prize. But the detail isn't anachronistic. Well, stylistically, perhaps, but not factually. We did wash and dry ourselves, after all, even in those long-ago days. And we did other things too. You never know how far I'll let this newfound freedom take me.

To AN OUTSIDE observer, the scene at that night's dinner table might have offered a prime occasion for comedy. Its participants, immersed in their own concerns, could not begin to see the humor of the situation, and that, indeed, would have made it all the more amusing to the imagined spectator. Roderick, for one, kept fussing about Antonio's projected arrival: Would it come off after all? And if so, when? Would he arrive in time for the larger dinner party planned for the morrow? And if he did, would he behave himself? The anticipatory host became so anxious over these questions, which he reiterated to Charlotte during the meal, that he perhaps took more wine than was good for him. He, at any rate, barely tasted the food.

In this he was lucky. Having made, with no help from the grime-covered household, an effort to dress for dinner, Charlotte now sat at the far end of Roderick's ridiculously long dining table, attired in her Worth dress and eating flour-paste. Surely that's what it was, this oddly congealed glutinous material in the soup bowl before her: flour-paste with a touch of herbal flavoring. Pierce had brought it in and set it in front of her. (Pierce, at least, had eventually materialized and duly dispatched her telegram to Lewis—that is, she trusted he had dispatched it.) But even he must have known something was amiss with the soup, for he vanished the moment his task was completed. Roderick, as usual, seemed not to notice the food. The wine, she had to admit, was quite good, but one couldn't dine on wine alone.

"You're really planning to give a large dinner party tomorrow night?" she responded to one of Roderick's anxious musings, hoping that her own anxiety had not been too rudely expressed in the interrogatory squeak she gave to the final word.

"Well, yes, that is, I had thought—to celebrate, you know, the arrival—friends from near and far, and all that." He was well into his cups by this time.

Charlotte, meanwhile, had picked at her overdone fish course (what *was* that fish? some kind of plaice, perhaps?) and was waiting, with a mixture of dread and hope, for the main course. She set down her fork. "Yes, well, in that case I think I'd better help you see to the arrangements. The kitchen—"

At that moment Pierce reappeared, without, however, bearing in any new dishes. He began to clear her soggy plateful away.

"Pierce!" she said.

Roderick looked up sharply from his napkin, which he had been tracing with the tip of his knife, forming temporary crisscrosses in the cloth as it lay folded beside his plate. It was not done, in his household, for guests to speak directly to the help, and he was surprised at Charlotte's violation of this old and honored rule.

"Yes, mum?" Pierce raised his eyes from her plate, but not to the level of her own eyes; his gaze hovered in the vicinity of her chin, as if prevented by brute force from rising any higher.

"How's Mrs. Pierce?" Charlotte began. She thought, in the brief moment he had spoken to her, that she detected alcohol on Pierce's breath.

"Fine, mum," he said, and scurried away before she could continue, leaving Roderick's plate uncleared.

"What was that all about?" her host growled.

"Well, I haven't seen the woman since I arrived, and if you're having guests for dinner tomorrow—"

"When does one ever see her? She's a creature of the subterranean regions, who feels at home only in the dark. Though I daresay she comes out to juggle with the china and dance on the tabletops when we've gone up to bed."

Charlotte charitably ignored his effort at humor. "At any rate, some organizing of the staff will have to be done, and rather quickly, if we're not to have a disaster on our hands tomorrow."

"And you're the very woman to do it, W.D. I place myself entirely in your capable hands. And now, if you'll excuse me, I must retire. I fear I've rather let the wine go to my head. Good night, my dear. Sit up as late as you like. Pierce will keep the fire going for you."

As he spoke, Roderick moved toward the door with a step that in any less dignified man might have been described as a lurching shamble. He disappeared, and Charlotte threw her napkin onto the table in a melodramatic gesture of despair. The gesture was for herself alone; it did not matter to her that there was no actual spectator to appreciate it.

"It's from Lewis," said Charlotte about the note that had slipped through the mail slot with the morning's first post, prior to any stirrings either upstairs or down. The small white missive carrying her own name above Roderick's address was still on the doormat when Charlotte came down, and since her host appeared just as she was tearing it open, she made its contents known to him immediately. "She'll be arriving on the 10:10."

"Splendid. Then she'll be well in time to give the Pierces a hand with tonight's dinner arrangements."

Charlotte suspected that a hand alone would be anatomically insufficient, but she kept this suspicion to herself. Roderick looked rather the worse for his bout with the previous evening's dinner wine, and she wanted to give him an hour or so to recover before springing any more worries on him. It was with this plan in mind that she sat him down to the breakfast tea Pierce had slapdashedly laid out.

But circumstances were not to favor her plan, for she had barely poured out their first cups when a knock at the door sounded.

"Who—?" muttered Roderick. "Pierce! Pierce! The door! Oh, for God's sake. Where is everybody this morning? Do excuse me, my dear. I'll just go get it myself."

She heard him open the door in the hallway and gasp slightly with surprise. His own hesitation, however, was more than countered by the bounding enthusiasm of the voice which greeted him in the warm, vibrant tones of a southerly clime. As Charlotte heard the interchange, she envisioned a large, jolly sheepdog, or perhaps some sort of energetic retriever, leaping up with pleasure to lick the face of a somewhat daunted but nonetheless proud owner.

"Good morning, good morning, Roderigo! Such a beautiful day, is it not?"

"Antonio! My dear boy. What a—I mean, how did you get here? We're miles from the station. We intended to—"

"I walked, of course! On such a beautiful day, it would be a crime not to. And see, such a little bag as I was carrying—there, I will put it on this little bench—it did not weigh me down at all." By this time they had appeared in the doorway of the breakfast room, from which Charlotte could see Antonio making his expansive gestures of affection and enthusiasm. Why *will* they insist on throwing their arms about like that, she thought, as if they were comic-opera figures?

"Good morning, Antonio," she said coolly from her place at the table.

"Ah, Charlotte, how charming!" He rushed over to kiss her hand, which she yielded to him with a barely discernible flicker of condescending amusement. *She* thought it barely discernible, but Roderick responded to it with a frown of irritation. "I did not expect, when I offered to make my visit to Roderigo's beautiful English house, that I should have the added pleasure of seeing you in it too."

"Oh, yes, it's apparently to be quite a house party, with a gala dinner tonight."

"Well, not—" But Roderick's demurral was stifled at birth.

"How lovely! A party for me? To welcome the arrival?"

"Well, actually—"

Charlotte stepped in this time. "A long-planned event, Antonio. But with you here it will be an even more festive occasion."

"—just a few of the neighbors," Roderick had gone on muttering, as if to nobody in particular. "Nothing out of the ordinary, but it will offer a fair sampling of the quiet life we lead here, and the kind of small entertainment we occasionally cook up for ourselves between long periods of solitary labor."

"Oh, yes, Roderick, for you the work, always the work is first." Antonio patted him heartily on the back. "A good policy. I only wish I could put it in effect myself."

Roderick did not dignify this wish with a reply, except to glance quickly in Charlotte's direction, and then to look guiltily away when she caught his eye. They had never discussed it in so many words, but she knew, and he knew she knew, that he had serious reservations about Antonio's "work."

"Well." Charlotte glanced at her watch, though whether in a conscious effort to break the uncomfortable silence or because she truly felt the pressure of time, Roderick could not be sure. "It's almost time for someone to go pick up Lewis at the station. Do you think Pierce can be trusted with the task?"

"Never mind, my dear, we won't bother to ask him. I'll go myself. I could use the fresh air."

"And I will accompany you," announced Antonio, flinging his palm against his chest in what Charlotte considered an unnecessarily emotional manner. "Thus we will have a chance to exchange our news during the ride, and the dear lady will not be bored by discussion of people she does not know."

"Most gratified, I'm sure," she muttered in her best imitation of a Cockney accent, earning another frown—but couldn't she discern a suppressed smile behind it?—from the ever-chastening Roderick.

"So delightful to be on English soil again at long last," she heard Antonio say as the two men moved toward the front door. "I have not been here since the Queen had her Golden Jubilee, and I was a mere boy traveling with my mother to see the great spectacle. How *is* your dear Queen, by the way?"

"Not too well, I believe, but thank you for your concern." And this time, in the wryness of Roderick's tone, Charlotte was sure she heard a conspiratorial answer to her own amused smile.

SHE'S NOT GETTING much better, is she? I thought that as time wore on you might at least begin to be charmed by Charlotte's peculiar sense of humor, but I'm afraid that even I don't find her terribly charming, and if not I, then who? Perhaps we must seek for interest in her striking absence of charm, her resistance (unwilled though it may be) to the conventions governing the charming heroine.

Not that Antonio is any better. But of course his charm is transparently ineffectual. Now, all these years later, I wonder for the first time if that was intentional on his part.

And I also, again for the first time, begin to perceive that Charlotte's evident disgust for Antonio (here I must stress the third-person formulation) may have been rooted in something quite the opposite. She found him repulsive, I mean, because she found him attractive. Those features that she might, in her inimitable fashion, have described as "oily" and "reptilian"— the smooth black hair, the large and seemingly pupil-less dark eyes, the skin the color of a Masaccio figure's—have come to be recognized, these days, as matinee-idol good looks. I, at least, can so recognize them; Charlotte was both too hard and too innocent.

She was uncommonly resistant to purely physical evidence. You'll notice that she hardly ever took in what someone or something *looked* like. If she remarked at all on appearance (or taste, or smell, or anything else reeking of the senses), it was only in order to comment immediately on the significance of this information in light of her own consciousness. Charlotte had trouble granting the world a separate existence. In regard to pure sense data, she had no visceral response—or at least none that she could measure or acknowledge.

On the other hand, she also had a rationale for such exclusions. She was interested, she would often say, in the drama of human interaction. And drama (as she knew from her few feeble attempts at writing for the theater) is a form that rigorously excludes description. Dialogue is all that matters; in this form, speech must convey everything. If this results in a heightened, melodramatized, starkly unrealistic sense of events, so be it. Theater, she would have said in her own defense, is meant to be theatrical. This she learned, I imagine, from Roderick; this I learned, at any rate, from his original.

WITH THE MEN safely out the door, Charlotte resolved to get to the bottom of the mystery about Mrs. Pierce. Where was the woman, and why hadn't she shown her face? The skimpy breakfast—a few dried crusts of toast and the makings of tea—showed no evidence of a feminine hand in its preparation.

"Pierce?" she ventured. There was no response.

"Pierce!" Though louder, this call felt, if anything, more futile. It was as if she were alone in a house haunted by silent, unresponsive ghosts: she could feel their presence in the air, but that presence did nothing to mitigate her essential feeling of solitary isolation.

Action was obviously going to be required. Charlotte rose from her chair with the dignity of an Assistant Commissioner about to investigate a remiss underling—that was indeed how she pictured her bold project—and opened the door leading to the heretofore hidden domain of the underground kitchen. (Or, if not an Assistant Commissioner, then perhaps Alice, she thought to herself.)

What met her eye when she reached the bottom of the steep, narrow staircase was far more distressing than anything Charles Dodgson had ever imagined. In contrast to Alice's pristine if ultimately tear-filled room, the kitchen of Shepard House was a grime-encrusted, soot-filled, rotten-smelling, entirely unkempt catastrophe. Days if not weeks of unwashed dishes lined the greasy counters. The old iron stove (which was also, apparently, the room's only source of heat) looked dead and blackened, as if it had suffocated on its own smoke before finally gasping to a halt. Streaks of dirt and dried mud and heel-ground food made such intense patterns on the floor that it was impossible to determine the original material of which the flooring was composed, much less its color. And over the whole gloomy dungeon, made more gloomy by the fact that the single small, high window had been covered over in grimy cloth, lurked an unpleasant, indefinable, but distinctly organic odor.

Charlotte at first assumed that the room was uninhabited—that Mrs. Pierce had, as it were, made her escape, and that what now lay before her eyes was the singular result of that departure. But a few moments in the comparative darkness enabled her vision to adapt sufficiently for her to discern a shape moving slightly in the corner of the room. The movement was as slight as the rhythm of breath, no more; but as Charlotte approached the shape more closely, it gave a deep snort, or perhaps snore, and rolled over. She could see then that it was a woman, though a woman so matted and tangled and dirty, in hair, clothing, and limbs, that even her own sex might have wished to disown her.

"Eh! You shouldn't be down here, mum!" It was Pierce, who had just come up behind Charlotte—sneaked up, she was tempted to say—in the filthy kitchen.

"Well, Pierce, that's hardly an adequate response to the situation I see before me." Charlotte crossed her arms in front of her and clutched her elbows, as much for self-reassurance as to convey the proper degree of chilling severity. "What's unseen might remain unknown, I suppose you were thinking. But sooner or later we were bound to investigate, were we not? Especially once the effects of the downstairs dissolution had begun to permeate the upper reaches of the household."

"I don't know about any of that. I answer to Mr. Stephen, and he hasn't complained."

"Your employer wouldn't notice if the house fell down around him, as long as his study remained intact. And I say that without any disrespect: he's a great artist, and he possesses the great artist's characteristic abstraction. But it's all the more reason why you should be looking out for the practicalities. Really, Pierce, I'm ashamed of you, letting things get to this point when Roderick depends wholly on you to keep Shepard House running smoothly. And to have this happen now, with a house party in residence and a dinner party planned for tonight. It's just too much. How could you do this to him?"

"It's nothing I've done, mum. You can see that for yourself. It's what she hasn't done."

Pierce gestured toward the ragged bundle in the corner. Charlotte eyed it distastefully.

"Yes. Quite. But what ever made you think that a woman in this condition would be capable of managing the daily operations of a household, much less a formal dinner?"

"She's always come out of it before, mum. It's never lasted so long before."

"*What's* never lasted so long before?"

"The drunk, mum. She generally starts it about Christmas and tops it off at the New Year. Of course, Mr. Stephen's always away for the holidays, so it never troubles him. And then she's always right as rain within a few days. But this time it's been weeks. Over three weeks now. Three weeks with barely a bite taken, and never leaving this room, not to sleep, not to take a bath—"

"I had noticed."

"—or brush her hair or anything. Not that she was ever much of a one for brushing and washing. But before this she did at least get into her bed. It's all I can do to keep enough food in her so that she doesn't waste away."

"And the liquor? Where is she getting the gin, or wine, or whatever it is she drinks?"

"I can't rightly say, mum. It's not Mr. Stephen's, you can be sure of that. I'm the only one that keeps the keys to the wine cellar. She must have a supply of it hidden somewheres. I haven't been able to find out where this time, I've been so busy keeping things going on my own. You see, I didn't want it to come out—"

"Why ever not? Can't you see the woman needs to be taken away somewhere? To some hospital or whatever? There must be places for people in her condition."

"She wouldn't let me call the doctor, mum. And there are no 'places,' as you call them, for people like us. If she were a rich lady—"

"All right, Pierce, enough of that socialist claptrap—"

"Not meaning to be rude, mum, but if she were a rich lady," Pierce continued insistently, "there might be someplace for her to rest and recover, but the only hospital we can afford is the poor-house sick ward, and no wife of mine will ever be sent into that."

"Hm. Well." Charlotte sniffed vehemently, and then regretted it. She pulled out her handkerchief and held it against her face, but the delicate smell of her own toilet-water only combined sickeningly with the stench of the kitchen, making her feel increasingly likely to retch. "Come upstairs with me now, Pierce—I assume she can be left like this for a while longer?—and we'll see what we can do to avert further disaster."

By the time Roderick returned from the station with Antonio and the invaluable Lewis, Charlotte had at least succeeded in canceling the impending dinner party. She had plucked from Pierce's resistant brain the names of the other invited guests, dashed off apologetic but sufficiently lighthearted notes to all of them, and dispatched Pierce to deliver the messages around the neighborhood. Roderick would, she knew, forgive her highhandedness when he learned of the circumstances that gave rise to it.

"At last!" She greeted the trio from the doorstep as they alighted one by one from Roderick's cart. "I'm afraid I've discovered something rather shocking in your absence."

A student of human nature would no doubt have given a great deal to be able to freeze and examine at leisure the three physiognomies that now proceeded to exhibit themselves to her. Antonio treated the tale of her basement excavations as a good joke, his wide smile indicating that he was barely managing to hold in, through the exertion of good manners alone, an appreciative burst of laughter. Lewis looked serious, practical, and stolidly undismayed, as if ready to ask what the next step should be. And Roderick's face bore such a complex mixture of emotions—amazement, curiosity, and pity were the ones Charlotte could most easily identify—that for a moment even she, immersed though she was in her narrative, was tempted to halt her rendition simply in order to classify and evaluate them.

"And how—how long did you say this had been going on?" Roderick finally managed to croak (if such inarticulate tones could ever be said to emanate from such an articulate man).

"Well, in this intense condition, since about Christmas. But apparently it went on every year, practically under your nose, though your nose was always conveniently elsewhere during the height of the holiday festivities."

"I knew she drank a bit at New Year's—"

"That hardly describes what I saw in the kitchen. The woman is a complete derelict, and apparently has been for quite some time. The husband told me, under duress, that she hasn't actually been out of the building for three years! And when I asked him why not, he said she hasn't got the clothes to wear outdoors."

"But I thought I'd made her a regular clothing allowance—"

"You have, but she obviously spends it on drink. He says he doesn't know where she keeps it, but I wouldn't put it past him to be encouraging her on the sly. At the very least, he's allowed it to go on without stopping her, and without, of course, telling you, as he was morally and legally obliged to do."

Roderick sank into a chair and rested his head in his hands. "I'm glad I didn't know. No, it's hateful of me to say that. I should have made it my business to know. But what would I have done about it? What, for that matter, am I to do now?"

"Well, she must be tossed out, of course," chimed in Antonio, "and the husband too. Is this not what you think, Carlotta?"

She was chagrined to hear her own advice coming from such an unwelcome corner. "Well, certainly they must leave the place." Roderick started to interrupt, but she quieted him by placing her hand on his shoulder. "I had thought a hospital of some kind, but apparently . . . well, that's not a possibility, it seems. And of course we can't just chuck them out in the streets." Here she glared at Antonio, intimating her own moral superiority to his predictable disregard of the human decencies. "I gather there's a sister somewhere. The woman will simply have to take them in. Lewis, when Pierce gets back will you please get the details from him and make the necessary arrangements?"

"Yes, mum."

"And in the meantime you'd best go downstairs and survey the damage. There's quite a lot of work to be done, even without the dinner party," she said to her maid's departing back.

"How, without the dinner party?" Antonio's smile was instantly replaced by a frown. "We are not to have my dinner party?"

"It was not your party and no, I've canceled it."

"It was not your party either, to do such a thing. How could you, a guest in Roderigo's house, take upon yourself—"

"Quiet, both of you!" Roderick stood up, still clutching his forehead. He pulled his hands away, as if by pure force of will, and looked in distress from one guest to the other. Then he reached out and took each of them by the hand. "Oh, dear. I'm so sorry. How could I shout at you, my two dear friends, when in fact I'm so grateful to have you both with me, in this moment of otherwise dire disaster and insurmountable gloom?"

He smiled then at his own penchant for self-dramatization. "Well, I imagine these old eyes have not seen their gloomiest yet, nor these ears heard their direst. I'll recover. But I must be alone for a short time, to think and rest. Will you please excuse me?"

And as he walked down the hall, one could have heard, if one had been keeping pace with him, a low but insistent muttering, such as might in a religious person go with the telling of beads: "Oh, Pierce, poor Pierce, oh, my poor Pierce . . ."

ONE LONGS, NOW that it is too late, to know how "poor Pierce" himself took the events of that day. I am sorely struck, re-reading my account, by the absence of the Pierce perspective, as it were. There needs to be a voice, a sensibility, which speaks at the very least for the unfairly injured husband, if not for the inscrutable Mrs. Pierce herself. Certain emotions and perceptions, crucial to the ultimate significance of the tale, simply cannot be rendered through Charlotte's consciousness, or even through Roderick's more generous one. I know that now. But I have missed my chance. At the time, twenty-five years ago, I would not even have tried to hear that voice. Now I try, but I get only silence.

RODERICK'S DEPARTURE LEFT the room momentarily empty of conversation. Other noise intervened: the ticking of the old clock on the mantelpiece; the switch of a stick, recently plucked from a country lane, that Antonio was carelessly, mindlessly striking against his leg; the rustle of Charlotte's skirts as she nervously paced back and forth before the window. But these sounds only served to heighten the silence, emphasizing the uncomfortable absence of the human voice when coupled with the strained presence of two people.

Antonio had assumed an air which Charlotte could only characterize as off-duty charm. His best, she perceived, was slyly saved for Roderick; his second-best was evidently sufficient for her.

"Well, Carlotta, if we are to have no dinner party, we must anyway make our own amusements, no?"

"The name, as you well know, is Charlotte—if you can pronounce it, that is." Two could play at the vanishing-charm game. "And I don't know about you, but under the present circumstances I'm not planning to outstay my welcome. Roderick is ill-equipped to have guests when he's got no servants at all in the house, and as soon as Lewis has put things to rights a bit here, and found a girl in the village to come in on a daily basis, we'll be making a hasty departure. I suggest you do the same."

"Ah, Carlotta," and he let her see the merest flicker of an ironic grin, "but you and I are hardly in the same relation to Roderigo, are we not? You are perhaps just the country-house guest, but I have come from so far away, from another country. And he has not seen his dear boy for many months. It would be rude of me to leave him in this lurch. I shall stay

with him as long as he wants me—for weeks, if necessary—
and be his solid support and loyal friend."

Charlotte was so angry that she couldn't, for a moment,
answer. Instead she turned abruptly to the window and stood
looking out at the grey winter day, as if fascinated by a particularly gnarled old tree growing down at the foot of the garden. Having recovered herself, then, she turned back with a
sharp flick of her skirts and advanced toward Antonio as a
fully rigged man-of-war might bear down on a fragile, oblivious pleasure boat.

"His solid support, eh? And what exactly do you propose
to do for him? Clean house? Wait on table? Or perhaps you
fancy yourself in a higher capacity—the muse to his art? Will
you stand by trimming his pens for him, or perhaps offer to
take dictation when his frail wrist tires? Oh, I can imagine all
the lovely pictures you've composed for yourself, Antonio. But
it won't wash. The poor man needs practical help, and then
he needs solitude—neither of which you're remotely capable
of giving him."

Antonio, however, proved to be neither fragile nor oblivious. "Jealous, are we?" he answered, in a much better imitation of a Cockney than she had managed to render. His
Italianate mannerisms, even his Continental accent—in fact,
every laboriously displayed indicator of his foreign birth—
seemed suddenly to have dropped from him. "You do not fool
me for one moment, my dear lady. I know you cannot stand
the sight of me. And part of what disturbs you is that you are
not exactly sure *why* you can't stand the sight of me. You think

it is because I'm bad for Roderick, because I impose on him, because he makes sacrifices for me. But why shouldn't he? You yourself make sacrifices for him and find it quite acceptable, as does he. Why should he be above all that? It is precisely that he is *not* above all that which makes you so distressed, so frightened, so angry. For if he is capable of making sacrifices for me, why then will he only accept them from you, and not give anything back? Whom does he evidently love better? There's the rub, eh?"

"You comprehend nothing. He gives me a great deal back. You only perceive the most superficial level, the most obvious favors and returns. Of those, I've no doubt, you've garnered more than your fair share, being the squeaky wheel you are. But of what really matters—of what Roderick, and only Roderick, is capable of giving—I get more than you can imagine. You don't even begin to understand what makes Roderick a great man, which is also what makes him a great friend."

"Ah, there you deceive yourself, Charlotte. They are not the same at all, the great man and the great friend. In fact they are opposites, two completely separate individuals inhabiting the same body. The great man is the one who produces the books, and the great friend—well, he is a different person to each of us, no doubt, but he is as separate from the great man as you are or I am. They are mere housemates, you might say, accommodated uncomfortably but permanently under the same roof. The great man sees everything, knows everything . . . Look at those devastating perceptions in the novels. It would be a terror to have such a man as a friend. He would be forever seeing through you to your horrible little flaws. But the great friend: ah, that side of Roderick is a mere child, easily delighted, endlessly forgiving. Your problem, Charlotte, is that you only want to be friends with the great man. It is an impossible wish, an aim that can never be achieved; and in aiming for it to the exclusion of all else, you make yourself impervious to the great friend who is really there, the lovely, pleasure-giving child hidden within the old man."

"He is *not* old," she snapped.

"Come, we need have no pretense here. He is upstairs, probably asleep by now. He *is* old. And you are not so young yourself. So don't hold too tightly to your dream world, or your chance of seeing and grasping the real world will be gone before you know it. Nothing lasts forever."

"No, nothing, thank God, not even this seemingly endless conversation." And with that she swept out of the room.

The house had been restored to something approaching its normal condition. The Pierces had been dispatched to the obliging relative, Lewis had been hard at work for hours, and by early afternoon Charlotte was satisfied enough with the progress to allow herself a restorative walk to Cambridge and back. She had not encountered Antonio since that morning's unpleasantness, but she knew him to be skulking somewhere in the house, and that knowledge made her anxious to get out of it.

"Tell Roderick, if he asks, that I'll be back for tea," she told Lewis as she left.

The walk was as she always remembered it—soothing, unchanging, even beautiful in its quiet Cambridgeshire way.

The path along the Cam was a bit muddy, but she had prepared for it by changing into her outdoor boots, so the minor
inconvenience was far outweighed by the brisk pleasure of the
trudge. Coming into the great university town from its back
door, as it were, she first saw the spires of King's and Trinity
looming through the trees. Then she approached the ancient
buildings and walked along the Backs, crossing the little imitation Bridge of Sighs at St. John's to get out to the front of
the colleges and return by way of King's Parade. As she passed
through the great gates of King's College and stopped a moment to admire the Chapel, she allowed herself to wonder how
different her own life would have been if, instead of being the
woman she was, she had been born a man like Gilbert—or,
for that matter, virtually any of the Englishmen she knew—
who took for granted his education at a place like this. It's a
matter of being spoon-fed, she thought. It enables you to grow
strong on a rich diet, but you never learn to forage for yourself. Not that I've had to do much foraging, except on the
intellectual front. But there I truly have had to cook my own
meals. And very good ones they've turned out to be, I might
add.

With these thoughts warming her, she turned back toward
the Grantchester path and Shepard House. As she walked along
the river, dusk was falling over the flat Cambridgeshire fens, and
the quiet loveliness of the countryside overcame her much-
vaunted resistance to nature's charms and made her want to
weep. She wished she *could* weep a few comforting tears, for it
had been a trying, terrifying day. She could still recall, as if it

possessed her even now, the quivering rage with which she had left Antonio after their quarrel. And then there had been all that business about packing off the Pierces to Lincolnshire. It was all very daunting. But of course it had been her duty to hold up, her obligation to Roderick, if nothing else; and she had managed to do so without a single hint of flagging or despair. It was not only her duty. It was her pleasure to be this strong. And now there would be the relief of tea.

But she had not counted on the fact that Antonio would have the nerve, the unmitigated insolence, to present himself at this occasion. After all he had said to her, and about her, and about Roderick, how could he calmly sit there in the best drawing room chair, waiting for her to pour out? It was too much.

I AGREE. IT *is* too much. But not in the way she thinks. Where does she get these phrases like "unmitigated insolence" and "without a single hint of flagging or despair"? Even then, people didn't speak like that.

I think I know what's causing the problem. It's Charlotte herself. (This is her story, after all, her world-view, even when she herself isn't onstage—or so Roderick would argue.) She doesn't sound like a real person because she never thought of herself as a real person. Instead, she always saw herself as a character in some kind of dramatic rendering: a heightened sensibility in a heightened setting. Well, let her be. *I'm* certainly not going to help her out any more. I've long since given up on her. She'll have to "fend for herself," as Roderick would say.

Charlotte hesitated at the open doorway that led from the hallway to the drawing room, contemplating a silent return to her own room upstairs. But then Roderick appeared, dear, kind Roderick, and smiled at her in the tenderest way, as if to acknowledge the immeasurable assistance she'd been rendering him all day.

"Go on, my dear." With a courtly flourish, part old-fashioned gravity and part joke, he gestured her into the drawing room ahead of him. "You see, we're back to civilization as usual—thanks, no doubt, to your more than competent ministrations."

"Yes, Carlotta is a wonder at practical things, is she not?" Antonio's stage-Italian manner had returned; he was himself again.

"Thank you, Antonio," she said icily. "Such praise from such a source is high indeed."

Roderick directed his frown at the cake plate instead of at her. It was as if he had decided to ignore the evidence of his senses, to presume that no antagonism had been intended, and to preserve, with his willful ignorance, the little group's tenuous hold on civility.

"You've been out, Charlotte?" he inquired in an obvious and uncharacteristic effort at tea-table chatter.

"Yes, to Cambridge and back. I do love that walk."

"So do I. It always makes the verities seem even more eternal."

"You must show me the colleges, Roderigo," Antonio chimed in. "While I am here is the perfect opportunity to see their stately beauties."

"Of course, my dear boy." But Roderick looked ever so slightly taken aback—or at least so Charlotte interpreted his mild expression of surprise. And no wonder, she thought, with the impudent dog proposing to make an indefinite stay at such a juncture.

"I was telling Antonio," she said, "that perhaps now is not the best time for either of us to be paying you a long visit."

"Nonsense!" Roderick's animation seemed unfeigned. "As you can see, everything is just about back to normal already. With your Lewis's help, Pierce has evidently been able to set everything to rights quite quickly."

"Pierce had nothing to do with it," she responded drily. "He and Mrs. Pierce departed on the 12:20, en route to Nottingham."

At this Roderick's face did change. He paled noticeably and looked at her with a long, slow stare. "Do you mean to tell me Pierce is gone?"

"Of course he's gone. They left together. That woman was barely able to walk by herself, and in any case he knew it was his duty to go with her. He had his hands full, what with Mrs. Pierce and their luggage, but I'm sure he'll manage. Pierce is a capable enough fellow, when he needs to be."

"He left without saying goodbye?" Roderick seemed unable to absorb the obvious fact.

"Goodbye?" Charlotte was sincerely astonished. "After the way he let you down? Did you expect him to say goodbye, a servant departing under the most ignominious of circumstances? Even Pierce has more sense than that. Oh, don't worry, he was treated well. I paid them an extra month's wages, and no questions asked about the missing clothes allowance. He was grateful for small mercies. You needn't worry, he won't be back to trouble you."

"Trouble me?" It was all he could do to echo her last words. She feared the great mind might be going at last, unsettled by the day's shocking events. But his next words relieved her fear, even as they gave her new cause for distress. "Charlotte, this is too bad of you. Pierce has been with me for over a decade, and whatever his shortcomings as a butler or a valet, he was loyal and affectionate and he gave me all I asked of him. And now you've thrown him out without so much as a by-your-leave, without a penny to his name—"

"I told you, I gave him a month's wages, which was more than he deserved under the circumstances—"

"Without, as I say, a penny to his name," he continued implacably, "and nowhere to turn for another job. I wouldn't have let him go at all, unless he felt that Mrs. Pierce needed him—quite right, too, poor fellow, that was evidently where his duty lay. So I suppose he did have to leave. But for you to send him off without even giving me a chance to have a last word with him . . ."

"I'm sorry." She realized now, though it was too late, how seriously he took the whole matter. "But you were resting, and we didn't want to disturb you—"

"We? I had nothing to say in all this," interjected Antonio. "I am innocent."

"*I* didn't want to disturb you," she continued, "after all you'd been through. I thought you'd already suffered enough. I—" She faltered and fell silent.

Roderick looked down at his half-empty teacup and stirred the liquid, as if absentmindedly, with his spoon. He then lay the utensil carefully in the saucer, and the tiny clink of silver against china was the only sound in the room. The silence lengthened unbearably, and even Antonio seemed afraid to break it. Finally Roderick looked up at Charlotte again, and this time compassion—for her, she felt, as well as for Pierce—mingled in his face with weariness and distress.

"I know you always try to do the best for me." He reached out and took her hand. "But sometimes your efforts to preserve me from suffering are themselves the cause of further suffering. I can't be protected from life, Charlotte. It's my element, and if I'm lifted too far above it, as you try to lift me, I won't be able to breathe. You want to make for me, to shape with the pure force of your powerful will, a cosy little life without pain; but that kind of life doesn't deserve the name. It's only a kind of deadness."

This time the tears did burst through, the tears that had been unable to flow earlier that day by the river, and she fled the room. They heard her feet tapping up the stairs, and the quiet but firm sound of her bedroom door being closed, but they could hear no weeping. Even in her great anguish, she was not the sort of woman to sob out loud.

"Well!" Antonio was the first to break the silence. He leaned back into the comfortable chair and crossed one leg over the other, as if settling in for a long stay. "It seems the old girl isn't made of stone after all."

"Antonio! For one thing, Charlotte's age is—"

"Oh, Roderigo, I mean no harm. It is a term of affection, as you say. Though why I should express affection for a woman who so hates the sight of me, I can't say."

"Oh, but she—"

"You know she does. I don't want to hear you lie about it. She has already admitted as much to me in a strange little conversation we had earlier in the day—the very same conversation, in fact, in which she admitted to being in love with you."

Here Roderick stopped him with a sudden frown. "You must be mistaken. Charlotte would never—"

"Oh, but I think you know her less well than you imagine—less well, at least, than a disinterested observer like myself. Or perhaps you find it easier not to know her, if you wish to love her."

"I do not, as you put it, 'wish to love her,' whatever you may mean by that. The feelings I have for Charlotte are warm, innocent, and entirely explicable by her good character, her intelligence, her wit, and her loyalty. Which is more, perhaps, than I can say about my feelings for you, dear boy." Roderick ended on a note somewhere between a growl and a groan, which would have been sign enough, had Antonio been paying heed, that the subject was not a joking one.

"Ah, your feelings for me! That is another matter, of course. I am flattered to feel I did not hold our superior connection over Charlotte's head when she told me of her love for you. No, that would not have been gentlemanly. But perhaps I did hint that in me you find a meeting of the souls, of artists' souls."

Here Roderick spluttered, whether with laughter or bitterness it would have been difficult for an outsider to say. His subsequent remarks did little to clarify the question. "Artists' souls! My dear Antonio, you *do* flatter yourself, and about more than your gentlemanliness. In what sense do you consider yourself more of an artist than Charlotte?"

"Why, in the absolute creativity of my efforts, and in their divorce from the commercial life. Charlotte is a mere scribbler for the contemporary marketplace. I am a student of the eternal human form—no, if my most sensitive friends are to be believed, a master. Charlotte constructs her entertainments for society ladies to while away their spare hours. I create artworks for the ages. And you well know that the plastic arts are inherently reflective of the highest in human creativity, being linked to the generative forces of the deepest in man's soul; while the literary arts, which use for their substance normal speech, are therefore tinged with the shopworn necessities of daily conversation. Only lyric poetry, among the literary arts, rises above the quotidian. Only—" Antonio recollected himself and, more to the point, his audience. "Only lyric poetry and the most lyrical of prose, such as your own. But you know what I speak of, for you too are such an artist."

"I am nothing of the kind, if being such an artist means wallowing in self-congratulation and criticizing better artists for knowing their craft. Charlotte's work has a connection to the marketplace because people want to read it. Yours has none because no one wants to buy your sculptures. That fact alone is not to your moral credit. Good artists can blush unseen, yes, but simply being unrecognized does not in itself guarantee the quality of your art. Anyone who tells you otherwise is deceiving you for purposes of his own."

"Such as?"

"Such as retaining your affection, you charming boy. But though I have long acknowledged your charm, I have never, I hope, conveyed a false impression about my opinion of your work."

"And that opinion is?" Antonio's whole stance had altered. His legs uncrossed and firmly planted in front of him, his hands gripping the arms of the chair, he leaned forward with his entire upper body, a pose which combined the eagerness and aggression of a snake about to strike.

But Roderick, like a creature that knows itself to be protected by its own poison, ignored the threat. "I think you know."

"I want to hear you say it."

"Are you sure? I fear you might never speak to me again if I do."

Antonio gave him a cold stare. "Take courage, then. I insist on hearing it."

"Very well, my dear. I say it with regret, for you are a lovely boy and a vastly entertaining companion. But you are also—

and I think you suspect this yourself—a complete charlatan as an artist."

Antonio launched himself out of the deep chair in one smooth, athletic motion. He stood before Roderick with tousled hair and a flaming face, looking, if anything, handsomer than ever, as if he had been waiting for years to enact this one moment.

"I leave tonight. I go now to pack."

"As you wish."

But as Antonio strode toward the drawing room door, his otherwise dramatic exit was ruined by the sound of the doorbell. He hesitated a moment, undecided as to whether he was still obliged, as a guest, to behave politely in the presence of this new and as yet unknown visitor, or whether his moral outrage as an insulted artist exempted him. Curiosity finally won out and he hovered in the hallway as Roderick, muttering, "Who can it possibly be?", slowly went to answer the door.

"Gilbert!" Roderick's voice expressed his surprise and something more: his shock, it might be termed, at Gilbert's relatively wild appearance—relative, that is, to Gilbert's usual sartorial perfection. This man who could emerge from a hard day's hunt as if from his morning toilette looked, for once, flustered and even a bit disarrayed. "Gilbert, my boy, however did you get here?" Roderick peered past his guest through the open doorway, as if to catch a glimpse in the misty dark of a departing conveyance. But none met his eye.

"Walked from the station. Ran, really." It was not only Gilbert's windblown hair and loosened clothing that made him seem wild; his voice, too, had been reduced to a mere gasping pant. "Sorry—one minute—must just catch my breath." For a brief moment, he leaned forward with his hands resting on his knees, heaving deep breaths in a most uncharacteristic fashion. Then he straightened up with a sweet, dim, sad smile of apology on his face. "Do forgive me, Roderick. I'm so sorry to intrude uninvited."

"Nonsense, dear boy! No invitation is necessary. But why didn't you telegraph? We would have picked you up at the station."

"I tried to telegraph, but I couldn't get through. That's why I'm here, in fact. They said it would be hours before the telegraph lines were clear, with all the messages going back and forth. And I knew you and Charlotte would want to know—" Gilbert had entered the hallway, gestured in by Roderick's inviting arm. His sudden silence was the result of his having caught a glimpse of Antonio at the far end of the entrance hall. Roderick turned to follow his glance. He waited a moment for them to acknowledge each other and then, when they didn't, took his cue from their silence.

"A young friend of mine from Italy, Antonio della Rossa." Roderick spoke with a degree of theatrical formality that was excessive even for him. "I believe he was just leaving. But I hope not before being introduced to my very dear friend, Gilbert—"

"We've met," Antonio interrupted him.

"Pleased to meet you," Gilbert was saying simultaneously, as he extended his hand.

Roderick looked quickly from one to the other. They both looked at him, with what seemed purposeful blankness.

"Come," he said, "there's a fire in the drawing room. Come in to warm yourself and give us your news."

"Very sad news, I'm afraid. But where is Charlotte? I thought she'd be here. She told me—"

"She is. She's upstairs resting—a little indisposed at the moment. But I'm sure she'll be down for dinner. Can the news keep until then?"

"I'm afraid not, or I would have waited for the telegraph lines to clear. I thought you and Charlotte would want to know right away. It's the Queen."

"She's dead." Roderick's voice dropped with sadness. "I've been expecting it."

"Yes, we all have. Still, with all the expectation it comes unexpectedly as a shock. I know Charlotte will be distressed— and that too is why I felt I should come in person."

"A very old lady," remarked Antonio. "Why are you shocked? It happens to all."

"Spoken with the hardheartedness of youth." Gilbert smiled grimly.

"He doesn't really comprehend."

"No."

"Comprehend what?" Antonio's tone was mocking, challenging.

"That it's the end of an era," answered Roderick. "The turn of the century was as nothing compared to this."

"Well." Antonio, who had allowed himself to be briefly drawn to the fireside, now rose gracefully out of his chair, though this time with somewhat less energy than in the scene of out-rage he had enacted earlier. "You gentlemen no doubt have a long English past to reflect upon together, and I must be pack-ing my things to go. So I will take your leave to depart."

"*Beg* your leave, dear boy, or take leave *of* you, if you prefer that construction. There's no point in employing linguistic flourishes if you can't employ them masterfully."

"I believe you used to consider my little errors a great part of my charm."

"I say, am I interrupting something here?" Gilbert too leapt to his feet. "I was so anxious to deliver my news that I abso-lutely abandoned all civilized behavior. But it's really too rude of me to intrude in this way, and I'll just catch the next train back to London."

"On the contrary." Roderick, from deep in his chair, waved Gilbert back to his seat. "Antonio was on the verge of leaving just as you arrived. It is he who must rush to catch the next train."

"As you wish." Antonio clicked his heels together with a little mock bow, then turned abruptly and marched to the doorway without a backward glance. Once in the hall, how-ever, he paused before going up the stairs. He appeared to be examining the Whistler drypoint on the wall, as if he had never before appreciated its fine details.

"And Charlotte?" he heard Gilbert's voice say. "It isn't like her to be ill."

"Don't worry, my dear boy, she's not really ill," Roderick answered. "It's just that she and I have had a little quarrel, and she and Antonio, apparently, a worse one; and she's gone upstairs to get away from us both. I imagine she'll be down for dinner, no doubt with all her usual self-possession restored. She'll have the advantage of both of us, I'm sure."

"Do you think she'll be angry at seeing me?"

"Angry? Why ever should she be?"

"At seeing me here. She does rather prefer to keep me off on the side, especially where you're concerned."

"She feels I'll be shocked, poor dear. And for her sake I might indeed be tempted to act it. But in this case the gravity of the situation, I should think, frees us from the usual proprieties. I will, of course, give you separate bedrooms."

"We always do take them, even at the hotel. You know how she is."

"Yes, I do know. Of all of us, I fear she'll be the least able to adjust to the new order. You know what they say about the Prince—King Edward, I suppose we must call him now. Hardly the man to enforce a code of public morality."

"To put it mildly. But perhaps the burdens of monarchy will slow him down a bit."

Antonio had heard all he needed. He sprang up the stairs with a light, soundless step. To throw his few possessions into a bag took but a moment. Then, leaving his room in disarray, he paused outside Charlotte's door and tapped softly on it.

"Yes?" Her voice was quiet but clear.

"May I come in a moment?"

After the briefest of pauses, she opened the door herself, as if to verify that his was indeed the voice she had heard. Surprise joined with distaste in her expression.

"Why?"

"A few last words. I'm leaving now"—he lifted his bag to show her he spoke the truth—"and I thought we should not part as we did below."

"If you're afraid I'll insult you when we next meet in Rome, you know me very little. As long as we continue to have friends in common, I'll behave with reasonable politeness toward you in public. I can dissemble as well as you."

"Ah, I never doubted it. I have learned no less from the sudden arrival of your friend Gilbert, with his news."

"Gilbert?" At this Charlotte did pale, and fell back a few steps. Antonio seized the opportunity to move forward and close the door behind him.

"Yes. He begged pardon for violating the proprieties, but apparently felt that he could not hold back. And Roderick, though saddened and disappointed by his news, nonetheless seemed unsurprised. Almost as if he had expected as much, but was sorry to hear it was so. As if, I might say, he had been personally wounded."

Charlotte visibly cringed. "But why—how—? I can't understand why Gilbert would do this, absolutely out of the blue. Why should he come here unannounced, essentially uninvited, and stir things up in this way? It just doesn't make sense."

"You are surprised? That he should come to Roderick with his news, his news that so closely touches the present inhabitants of this house?"

"His 'news,' his 'news'—why do you keep saying that, you stupid boy? There is nothing 'new' about it, as I suppose you've already learned. You mean his information: that's the proper term for it in English. But *why*?" she wailed. "Why should he want to betray me, and to Roderick of all people? Well, if he wanted to betray me it *would* be to Roderick; he at least knows me that well." Having seemed, in the sudden sway of passion, to forget her audience entirely, she now acknowledged him directly. "But if he were going to give us away, why would he choose to do it in front of a meaningless stranger like *you*?" She narrowed her eyes at him. "He would never do that. You must be lying. How, then, did you know?"

Antonio's smile was wider than she had ever seen it. "The dear lady is rambling. I cannot imagine how this confusion occurred. Gilbert's news—and I believe that *is* the proper term—has to do with the death of your beloved Queen. He has dashed all the way down from London to be the first to announce it."

She would have fallen to the floor if he had not caught her. Lifting her up in his arms, Antonio settled her into the soft blue divan that occupied the center of the room, in front of the fire. She regained consciousness almost immediately, while he still had his arms around her, and she pulled back in horror—not so much at his touch, it seemed, as at the instant memory of what she had unwittingly told him. For the first time in their acquaintance, the disgust in her face was outweighed by fear.

"What have I done?" she whispered, attempting to pull back from him. But he cornered her in the chair.

"So it is not the Queen you mourn?" he sneered.

"Oh, the Queen! I will have time enough for her, in the years to come. But why? Why have you done this to me?"

"I have done nothing but save you from a bad fall. It was all your doing."

"You won't tell anyone? You won't tell *him?*" Immediately, he could see, she regretted begging the favor.

"How could it matter what I say—a stupid boy, a meaningless stranger?"

Charlotte bit her lip. "I spoke in anger. I was desperate."

"And now you've changed your opinion? You find in your heart a deep affection for me after all?"

She looked straight into his handsome, repellent face, inches away from hers. "No. I despise you."

At this he released her and stood up. "Good. At least you are still honest. That much character remains to you."

"You are a hateful cad. A gentleman would never use his advantage in this way."

"Come, Carlotta," he laughed. "We are far beyond the invocation of such rules. Surely I am not merely a 'cad,' as you so quaintly put it. I am the grand instrument of your fate. You, however, must take responsibility, for you are the musician who has given the instrument its tune."

"You flatter yourself. You are a mere accident. It could have been anyone."

"Could it?" he said. By this time he was at the door, one hand on the latch, the other boyishly swinging his bag. "I am not such a stranger, meaningless or otherwise, as you may think. Ask Gilbert about that. Ask him about the night in Trastevere, or the week in Venice. Then decide how much of an accident I am." And with that he was gone.

———

A lesser woman might have taken to her bed for the remainder of the evening and felt justifiably excused, but Charlotte was dressed, combed, and ready for a public appearance within thirty minutes of Antonio's departure. Having cashed in all her moral chips, as she put it to herself, she felt the freedom of the independently poor. Fate had handed her a share of exposure; very well, then, she would make it her own and brazen things out as far as she could. In her present state she felt that might be very far indeed.

"Gentlemen."

They looked up simultaneously from their cosy fireside, evidently surprised not only by the greeting itself but by *her* absence of surprise, and all that it implied.

"Charlotte, my dear, I'm so pleased you felt well enough to come down. Gilbert has joined us, as you see, with some very sad news—"

"I know. Antonio stopped to tell me, on his way out."

At this Gilbert gave her a sharp glance, which she returned. There had perhaps never been a sharper one between them.

"You'll be joining us for dinner?" she asked him.

"Roderick has kindly asked me. And then I'll be off first thing in the morning. I do apologize for intruding uninvited. You know that only the most serious circumstances could have forced me into such rashness. I knew you would want to hear immediately."

"We need no apologies here," she said quietly. "Roderick and I"—and here she cast an affectionate glance at the denominated individual—"have grown quite used to a certain lack of ceremony, I might almost say a frenzied state of uncertainty, at Shepard House. Things have been rather at sixes and sevens these last few days, as you've probably been told."

"I'd say thirteens and fourteens, at the very least," Roderick added. "Not, I'm afraid, the turn-of-the-century house party to which I intended to invite you, Charlotte. Can you forgive me?"

"There's nothing I couldn't forgive you, and you know it perfectly well."

Gilbert looked from one to the other, then hastily interrupted the silence. "Might you, too, be going back to London tomorrow, Charlotte? I understand the Funeral is to be quite soon"—her gaze, at this, locked with his—"and perhaps you'll want to return to London before then. I offer my services as an escort. That is, if Roderick has no further need of you here."

Roderick answered with a generously dismissive wave of his hand.

"Thank you, Gilbert, that's very kind," she said. "I don't know exactly how soon I'll leave, though under the circumstances I suppose it had better be quite soon. Can I let you know in the morning?"

"Of course."

Lewis came in to announce that a dinner of sorts had been prepared. She started with recognition when she saw Gilbert, then composed herself again into a mask of impersonality.

"As you can see, Lewis," said Charlotte, "we have an extra guest for dinner and for the night. Can you see that his room is prepared?"

"Yes, mum."

"What would we have done without you, Lewis?" Roderick warmly urged.

"What, indeed?" echoed Gilbert, more quietly. Charlotte gave him a quick look suggesting that more restraint was in order, and he smiled at her in what she considered an odd way.

After dinner—which was, Charlotte felt, a vast improvement over anything she had yet eaten at Roderick's table during this visit—their host excused himself, saying only that the day's events had worn him out completely. "I'll see you two in the morning. Please feel free to stay up as long as you like. Now that the fire is going so well, it would be a shame to waste it on an empty room."

"I imagine I'll be coming up soon myself, but thank you, dear," said Charlotte, giving his hand an affectionate squeeze.

"Goodnight, both of you." He smiled at them from the doorway, and then they heard his heavy tread retreating up the stairs.

They sat without speaking for a minute or two, watching the flames dance. It would have been out of character for either to make a sudden move in the direction of the other, whether physical or verbal; and circumstances compounded their normal reticence. Finally Gilbert cleared his throat.

"He knows."

"I know," she answered. "He tricked me into confirming it."

At this Gilbert looked more than surprised. "Tricked you? That seems entirely out of character."

"On the contrary, I'm afraid it's all too much in character. You no doubt judge him less harshly than I do, having your own reasons for being blinded."

"Blinded?" Gilbert seemed genuinely at sea.

"I mean your own prior relationship."

"Well, I may have met him before you did, but surely your connection with him is much closer—"

"How can you say that to me, knowing what you know?" She turned on him then, almost panting with suppressed rage. "I hardly know the man."

"Charlotte, calm yourself. You act as if you'd been betrayed in some way, but he would never do that to you. Perhaps your own regard for the social proprieties has caused you to misinterpret his feelings. He would never condemn you—"

"Oh, no, that's not what I'm afraid of. On the contrary, he will welcome me into his corrupt circle. He will trumpet to the world that I've fallen. He will, at the very least, tell my dearest friend, who will not be able to believe it at first and then, believing it, will realize that he's all along doubted my capacity for true self-sufficiency."

"Your dearest friend? I thought *I* was that."

She looked at him with a mixture of disbelief, pity, and contempt. "I mean Roderick, of course."

At the sound of the name Gilbert pulled up short. "Of whom have we been speaking?"

His confusion momentarily confused her. "When?"

"Just now. The man who tricked you, the man you hardly know. I thought—"

She gave a sharp laugh. "You thought it was *Roderick*?" Then her eyes widened. "Do you mean to tell me that *he* knows?"

"And has for a long time. He doesn't mind in the least, my dear. You really underestimate his capacity for sympathy and tolerance." He smiled and reached for her hand, which she withdrew quickly. The gesture seemed to return him to himself, and to his initial confusion. "But to whom, then, did *you* refer?"

"Can't you guess?" By this time she was so awash in shame and distress she felt she could risk anything. So Roderick had known all along, and yet had allowed her to continue the deception and self-deception. What a fool he must think her. What a fool she was.

"No," he answered, wonderingly.

"I suppose you never saw him before tonight?"

Gilbert blushed deeply. "Ah."

"And why did you never tell me?"

He shrugged. "There was nothing to tell."

"That's not what he says."

"I mean nothing of importance, nothing that affected you in any way."

"Anything that affects Roderick affects me."

"Oh, so you're only interested in protecting *him*?" Now he was on the offensive. "It's not your own interests that are at stake?"

"You flatter yourself."

He got up then and stood in front of the fire. When he spoke, his back was still turned to her.

"Charlotte, don't throw this away. You're speaking in anger now, and it makes you cruel. Give yourself a few hours to calm down. By tomorrow it will all seem to be nothing."

"It *is* nothing, already. It has been nothing for years, only I've refused to acknowledge it."

He turned to her then, and there were tears in his beautiful eyes. "You only make it nothing by saying so."

"I only tell the truth."

"Ah, Charlotte, you have always been too certain of your truths. And the world has conspired with you by supporting you in them. But that world is dying out now, and certainty won't always be the virtue you think it is. Let it go, Charlotte. For once, allow yourself to be in doubt. A part of you longs for it."

"You know nothing about me," she said angrily.

"I know enough about you to know that you will never forgive me for knowing even as much as I do." He picked up her hand then—this time she let him—and tenderly kissed the palm. "It was not nothing." The tears started to her eyes then, but he was out of the room before they could be seen.

She couldn't be sure how much time she had passed alone in front of the fire: enough, at any rate, for the coals to smoulder almost into ash. But she at long last did come to herself (that was the exact manner in which she saw it, as a return from a long journey elsewhere, away from the person she really felt herself to be) and at that point she went up to bed. Pausing by Roderick's door, she saw a thin light shining under it, and this emboldened her to knock, despite the lateness of the hour.

"Come in, my dear," said his familiar voice.

"How did you know it was I?" she responded as she entered, closing the door behind her.

"I could say that it was an appropriate greeting for either of you, and that would be *a* truth, but not *the* truth, which is that I long ago heard Gilbert making his preparations for sleep." He nodded at the far wall, which separated his room from the guest room in which he—or rather, Lewis—had put Gilbert. It had not escaped his notice, but only his commentary, that Charlotte's room lay, through connecting doors, on the far side of that one.

"Why are you up so late?" Charlotte's face expressed affectionate concern.

"I might ask you the same thing. I, at least, have the excuse of a good companion." He held up the leatherbound volume from which he'd been reading when she entered.

She took the only other comfortable chair in the room; they were close enough, familiar enough, that she did not expect to wait until he offered it, and he did not expect to have to. She rested her head against the profusion of flowered upholstery and closed her eyes.

"I'm very tired."

"It's been a tiring day," he agreed, his tone hanging fire as if in expectation of something more—as if he were opening, not closing, the subject under discussion.

"I've had two quarrels."

"Are you counting the one with me?" he asked gently.

At this she opened her eyes. "Did we quarrel?"

"Over Pierce."

"Oh, yes." She paused, whether in remorse or simply in recollection he couldn't be sure. "Have you forgiven me?"

"You know there's no need to ask."

She took it, as he meant her to, as a general dispensation for all sins past and future.

"How did you come by it, this largeness of yours?" she presently said.

"I take it you don't allude to my girth."

She smiled. "You know perfectly well what I mean. How do you remain so dispassionate about all of us tiny mortals? You seem to care about us individually well enough, but your tolerance is almost inhuman, as if we were finally incapable of offending you. Where does that come from?"

"Ah." He spread his hands in disclaimer. "If I knew the answer to that, I would probably cease to write. Perhaps to live."

"But you do care about us?"

"Of course."

"Some more than others?"

At this he eyed her warily. "Be careful, my dear."

"But doesn't every child wonder if she's the most loved?"

"Oh, Charlotte. How can I answer? I am a man of detachments, of removals and evasions. With you, perhaps, I feel most myself—which is also to say that with you I feel most detached and removed. Is that passionate preference, or its opposite?"

"I don't ask you for passion."

"No, and I don't give it; it's not, at any rate, my best emotion."

"Did you know about Gilbert and Antonio?" She suddenly changed tack.

"Yes," he answered, without a glimmer of surprise or discomfort. She had once again, she realized, underestimated him. Not only was he above the human fray; he was so far above it that the peripheral skirmishes did nothing to alter his sense of essential character. Other people's attachments, whether physical or purely emotional, were of little importance to him, except insofar as they bore on his understanding of the human mechanism in general. So, at least, she interpreted his calmness. But if he could accept Gilbert's peccadillos so easily, why not hers? What made her think he expected more of her in this regard? Perhaps it was only that she wished him to expect more of her; perhaps the higher expectations were all hers.

"Why didn't you tell me?"

"About Gilbert and Antonio?" But she knew, as he spoke, that he meant another pair as well. "Would you really have wanted me to tell you that I knew? Let me put it another way: would you really have wanted *me* to tell you?"

"No," she agreed. "I couldn't have borne it from you. I could hardly bear it from Antonio, even though I despise him completely."

"Now, now."

"But he is despicable, Roderick, and not at all worthy of— of a man like—"

She stopped here, afraid to go on. There had been enough revelation for one evening. Charlotte was fearful that even a single additional fact, teetering on the pile of unwelcome knowledge, might bring the whole structure crashing down. Unspokenness had always been her way with Roderick; best to let that prevail now. It was certainly the mode *he* would prefer to adopt, as he indicated by failing to take up her aborted comment, instead letting the silence between them lengthen into a natural, companionable pause.

And yet she wanted to know. For possibly the first time in her relation to Roderick, she was aware of longing for more than had been granted to her. Roderick's "interest" in handsome young men—oh, she had been willing enough to allude to it in passing, to grant him his preferences of one bodily type over another, as if it were all a purely aesthetic exercise, like the contemplation of Greek sculpture. But when she allowed this line of thought to develop itself fully, it frightened her. For if Roderick had allowed himself *his* passions, then for what earthly purpose had she been denying hers? And that question led her almost to the brink of a further one, about herself and Roderick. But to make the question explicit, to formulate it anywhere but in the deepest abysses of dream-induced consciousness, would be to violate everything they had so delicately cultivated over the years. Tonight, at any rate, was not the proper moment for such importunities. Perhaps tomorrow morning she would have the courage to ask him. Or perhaps not.

She placed her hands on the armrests, then, in preparation for rising. "Shall I go back to London tomorrow?" she asked. "Or do you need me here?"

"One always needs you, Charlotte, but it is best to learn to do without. I would find it all too easy to allow you to run my entire life for me. And then what would become of your own writing?"

"Oh, that." This time it was she who was dismissive.

"That indeed," he insisted gently. "You have a task to do that no one can do better."

"I suppose so. Oh, don't worry, I'm in no danger of giving it up. I'm like the workhorse who continues to make his rounds even after he's been retired; it's not in me to stop. But I do sometimes get bored with my little pasture, and wish for larger fields. *Your* fields, for instance."

"Oh, *my* fields." He seemed to mock his aspirations even as he affirmed them. "They are hardly spacious. In fact, they seem to me to get smaller and smaller every year."

"Mines, then, not fields: as you draw inward, you go downward, deeper than anyone else."

"And strike gold, eh? Or is it just dirt and stone? I wish I knew. But thank you, my dear. Your confidence, I sometimes feel, takes the place of my own."

She rose. "Will you go to bed now?"

"Not quite yet." He smiled. "You have given me some ideas, and I think I'll spend a while in my study."

"Not too late," she warned.

"Yes, *mater*," he laughed. But long after she had fallen asleep in the room next to Gilbert's, he was still at his desk, writing.

I HAD FORGOTTEN how cold it can get in this country. I just now took a walk in the park. It looked so inviting outside my window, and hard as I had tried, I wasn't getting any closer to producing a speech. (Well, perhaps it was because what I was trying hard at wasn't speechwriting. I was remembering; and not necessarily useful memories, at that.) I thought the fresh winter air might clear my head. But I didn't really dress warmly enough. Oh, I had a muff, and my coat, and even a woolen scarf for my head. But the wind seemed to whistle right through them all. Very penetrating, that New York wind.

I hadn't been aware, until I went out, how overheated the hotel room was. Overlit as well: the electric glare is everywhere in this country. (Though I'm grateful enough for that in the evenings. My night vision, never very good, has worsened with age.) At any rate, my excursion in the park was illuminated only by plain, old-fashioned daylight. And I did enjoy my walk around the frozen lake. It's a lovely setting, in the snow, with the bare trees and the gently sloping hillsides; you would hardly imagine you were in the midst of a vast city. A number of young courting couples seemed to find it quite a romantic place to walk and talk. Or perhaps they were young marrieds anxiously discussing household cares. I can no longer tell at a glance, if I ever could.

As I hurried back, my face now grown numb from the wind, I nearly laughed at the sight of the hotel's endearingly grandiose façade. That German-wedding-cake, Rhine-palace look, with those little corner towers and their green-tinted roofs. All that heavy stone and glass and shiny metal, attempting to add up to a monument and failing dismally. Why do recent American buildings try so hard to look like their European ancestors, when they would do so much better to strike out on their own path? Pastiche is always undignified, even when what it imitates is the embodiment of dignity.

Still, it's a pleasant enough hotel, and it does its essential job, which is to keep me warm and comfortable. I don't know why it feels so much colder in New York. It's not as if we were never cold in France, especially during the War, with the fuel shortage. But I'm absolutely certain the wind at home was never that piercing, even during the War. Or am I? So many of these things are colored by temperament rather than fact. Our temperaments, I suspect, were more resistant in those days, or at least mine was. We just didn't notice the outside world as much, or perhaps we willfully chose not to notice.

The War did break our hearts, though. I remember the letter I got from Roderick in August of 1914. He had written it the day war was declared, from Shepard House, of course— that late in life he could hardly be budged from home. I was at home myself, in France, when I got his letter, and I can still remember its opening sentence. "The plunge of civilization into this abyss of blood and darkness," he wrote, "is a thing that so gives away the whole long age during which we have supposed the world to be, with whatever abatement, gradually bettering, that to have to take it all now for what the treacherous years were all the while making for and *meaning* is too tragic for any words." How like him to use so many words and then say that any were useless. But how like him, also, to get it essentially right. We did, after 1914, suddenly see the whole blithe period beforehand as a foolish, empty preliminary to this terrible outburst. While we were living through it, we thought it was progress, or at worst daily life. Instead it turned out to be trouble silently brewing, secretly heading toward tragedy.

That's the way with hindsight, of course. It telescopes the past, makes it go by in a flash: brief because, in retrospect, causally meaningful. It's a shame we only get the sense of perspective when it's over. Or perhaps it's a blessing.

Odd that Roderick should have been so quick to pick up the significance of this particular event, though, because we never thought of him as a man of political sensibility. After the Queen died (Queen Victoria, of course I mean—*our* Queen), he rather lost interest in affairs of state. Only the domestic and the local seemed to matter to him. He would be laughing now if he could hear that yesterday I received a telegram from the President of the United States, congratulating me on my prize. Not that this one's much of a president, really—but then none of them has been, since TR. He was the last grand figure, the last who thought of himself in grand terms.

Now I *am* sounding like Roderick, with his outdated affection for the old, dead Queen. We younger people rather mocked him for it, even as we shared his sentiments. ("We" younger people, indeed; he would never have let me advertise my few years' advantage so flagrantly. But then, I never would have done so, to his face.)

Perhaps what made him lose interest wasn't the Queen's death at all. Perhaps—it's the first time I've thought of this, really—perhaps it was the public reaction to the novel he was working on when she died, that winter of 1901. He was in the midst of it, I imagine, when we were all there for that dreadful business with Pierce. Not that he told me this; he would never actually say what he was working on. But he was definitely writing *something*, and this was the next book of his to come out, after the Queen's death. Very badly received it was, too. People (to the extent "people" wanted him to do anything— his sales were never enormous) wanted him to keep writing the same sort of thing he had always written: sophisticated, subtle, domestic tragi-comedies, with princes and princesses and actresses and wealthy collectors, in Venetian palaces and London mansions and Paris hotels. They didn't want to hear from him about the servant class. They didn't want to hear from him about madness and cruelty and drunken behavior. Above all, they didn't want to hear from him about the future, or at least his image of the future. The critics savaged Roderick's "failed experiment" (I believe they even compared it unfavorably to second-rate H. G. Wells), the marketplace turned up its collective nose, and the book sat unbought on the bookstore shelves. Roderick was so dismayed by the public response that he renounced the novel; at any rate, he omitted it from the Complete Edition and never allowed it to be reprinted in his lifetime.

Death has an odd effect on a friendship. You don't stop being friends with a person just because he's dead. But one half of the relationship freezes. Roderick today is exactly the same as he was ten years ago, when he died, whereas I . . . I have been forced to adapt to the world. The world *has* changed, if not exactly in the way he predicted—and so have I. But he is the same, growing ever younger by comparison as I grow older. Soon I will pass him by, and he will dwindle to a mere youth from my antique perspective.

The conversation, too, becomes frustratingly one-sided after death. I still talk to Roderick, in my mind, but he never answers me. Or rather, he answers only in the form I can retain of him, which grows increasingly thin and ghostly. Hard as I try, I cannot intensify him; I cannot bring him up in full, fleshly solidity. I used, when he had just died, to be able to hear his voice in my ear during these imaginary conversations. But I no longer can. His responses, when I can manufacture them, are incorporeal, like writing. They have no timbre, no human inflection.

I suppose this is the merciful adjunct to bereavement. We would not be able to live if we carried our dead too fully with us; they would weigh us down, immobilize us. At first, I've noticed, it is the grief itself we cling to. That passion seems the last real remnant we'll ever have of our relation to the beloved dead, and we're loath to let it go. But then even the grief starts to dissipate. Its presence ceases to be daily, constant, solid. It too becomes ghostly.

I wonder if, having had children, one would feel so strongly about one's dead. Possibly not. At times I wish I *had* borne a child, and raised it, and seen it grow to adulthood. It would be nice to think of a life continuing after mine. Yes, that would have been a deep pleasure. It never seemed something I would want until it was too late. And even then . . . I've always had too many doubts. Children seem to demand such certainty. Even *men* seemed to demand more certainty than I was usually willing to give.

Except Gilbert. Except Gilbert. He was right when he said to me that it was not nothing. (Odd, isn't it, how some truths can only be expressed in a double negative.) He was wrong, though, when he said I would never forgive myself. I did eventually forgive myself, and him as well. Oh, it was too late for us to start over. It was *always* too late for us, I suspect, even when we first met. But we became good friends—"again," I almost said, except that lovers aren't really friends. Gilbert and I became real friends, and even after he married (yes, he did marry, a nice enough woman, if a bit of a ninny), we kept up our correspondence and our annual visits. I suppose I would have to say that after Roderick, he was my best friend. If Gilbert hadn't died last year, I expect he would have come to New York (though he loathed New York) just to see me get this silly prize.

I *am* getting maudlin. An old woman's privilege. Or a very young one's. Funny how life seems circular in that way. We try for so long to grow up, to acquire the trappings of adulthood, and then when we've got there we do our best to retreat back to childhood. I think it's intentional: old people want to be babied, so they act like children. It's not deterioration of the brain or anything biological like that. It's a willed effort on their part. On my part.

I don't want to leave, though, without leaving something behind. A child would have been nice. People say books can be like children, but mine don't feel that way to me. Books are like my *revenants*, my dear dead friends: they are only alive as long as someone is thinking about them.

Perhaps my books will someday bring me a child of sorts, an imaginary descendant, reading what I've written and conjuring me back to ghostly life. I would like that. She would be my future, and I would be her past, even though no ties of blood bound us.

A fanciful idea, worthy of Roderick's declining years. But that's as much as I would ever hope for—to be worthy of him, even at the end. He taught me, after all, everything useful I ever knew about love, and about work; what he taught me, really, is that work *is* love, transmuted. You take the wishes and desires and longings and hopes you've gleaned from wanting other people, and you turn them into something you can use yourself. And when you've made of those feelings something that can go back out into the world, that other people can respond to and care for, then the transformation goes the other way, and work becomes love.

He sat, then, long after she had left his room, occasionally pausing to rest his cramped fingers, but otherwise scribbling madly, as if his life depended on it. That was the very figure of speech which came self-mockingly to his mind, and he grimaced at his own pomposity, his own eternally clamoring sense of self-importance. And yet where was the fiction to come from, if not from that domineering, unrelenting, overweening, impossible self?

Even that turn of the screw, however, struck him as insufficiently tight, for the real point was that the self had to disappear—had to be there to set the thing going, as it were, and then quietly bow out. Like a playwright, perhaps; or a Jansenist's vision of God. Which similarity (it occurred to him now for the first time) might well explain the affinities between Racine and *his* God. The absent creator: a nice little idea for an essay on the French dramatists. Well, but there would be plenty of time for that sort of thing when he was finished with this undertaking, which in the meantime would keep him busy for as long as his supply of energy (and the smooth functioning of his household—let him not again be unaware of that) held up.

She had given him, without knowing it, an idea—not in anything she said so much as in the view she had taken of her work, and his, and their respective lives, together and apart. It was this, precisely, which had been missing from the project thus far. He had neglected his own best advice: the importance, that is to say, which he always attributed to the perceiving consciousness. In this case it would be, as well, an envisioning consciousness, a sensibility capable of peering into the future as well as chronicling the past (and, not least, reflecting on the present).

It would, of course, be a female sensibility, for the feminine muse had always served him best, rendered him the most loyal assistance, kept him most firmly on course. (Except, he was forced to admit, in the case of Mrs. Pierce. He had rather missed the target there.) So she, the narrating figure— or as close to narrating as made no difference, whatever the grammatical forms might be—would be a woman. Probably a young woman: a girl just on the precipice of adulthood.

Or would it be possible, just this once, to have her be both old *and* young? He contemplated with some sadness, here, the fact that one is inevitably trapped in one's own moment of history, limited to one's own time. Imagine the pleasure, if one could accomplish it, of living in more than one era. Though would it indeed be a pleasure, or merely the source of additional pain? In either eventuality, the possibilities for fiction might be fruitfully expanded. To experience hindsight and foresight all at once: to have the panorama of the whole human life spread before one, and still to have the delicious sense of embarking on an unknown voyage . . . That indeed would be something.

He would, at any rate, give it a try; he would, in the language of the jocular young men, do his damnedest. He could see it all, now, exactly before him, down to the minutest details of dress and gesture. The beginning would have to be redone, now that he had at last seen the way clear before him. He would have to go back when he was finished and trim the unwanted brush, allowing the sprig to grow straight and true. But the thing had a life of its own now, and he needed to honor that.

Formerly the story's maker, he had become its scribe. It was his task now simply to listen to the voice and get it all down intact. And where that voice came from—bits of Charlotte's cherished conversation, the personalities of his other friends and followers, household events, his own entire youth and early adulthood—none of this mattered now; it was none of his business. All the little shoots, wherever they had started, would somehow grow into a single tall tree.

Or perhaps (he could never, he castigated himself mildly, rest contentedly with his figures of speech, but needed to be always pruning and tinkering), perhaps it wasn't a tree after all, but a tower: something like the Chinese pagoda at Kew Gardens, of which he had always been so fond. Now *there* was an image to work with. He would bequeath it to her, leave it as a ghostly gift to his charming muse, his Charlotte-sprung girl, his still unnamed, unknown descendant.

Book Two
1956

IN THOSE YEARS, and in that place, everyone gave a certain sort of dinner party. It began, perhaps, with cold cucumber soup, moved on to a roast, and then to a particularly unappetizing salad, which was in turn succeeded by a sweet, heavy, baked dessert. The meal was always preceded by drinks—generally martinis or, for the ladies, gin-and-tonics; the repast itself was then accompanied by randomly selected French wines and followed by sticky liqueurs. Sometimes the men smoked cigars afterward, while the women cleared the table and stacked the dishes on the drainboard, leaving the washing and drying to be dealt with by the wife after the guests had gone home.

Because the town was isolated and academic, and the American expatriate community even more so, there was a limited pool of potential guests and a correspondingly high level of conversational tedium. Which was why Sarah was so surprised, the night of the Gardners' dinner party, to find herself enjoying the evening. On one side of her sat red-faced Herb Lingman, with whom she routinely fought about politics. ("I'm madly for Adlai," she had responded this evening, when he tried to argue in favor of a second term for Ike. Neither side, in any case, had a hope of influencing the other, since they had already mailed off their absentee ballots.) And on the other side was a man she had never seen before. New blood. He was no doubt attached to the other stranger at the table, a woman seated at the far end from Sarah, next to their host. The woman was sharp-featured, sharp-eyed, and a bit dowdy, in the fashion of British lady professors. Her husband, if that's what he was, seemed much younger, barely more than a boy—perhaps twenty-six or twenty-seven at most, too young to be taken seriously. Sarah thought he was devastatingly handsome, which made her mistrust him.

"Aren't you the writer?" he asked her. "Sarah Jameson? We were told she would be here tonight, and by the process of elimination I've deduced she must be you."

Sarah surveyed the table and acknowledged, silently, that none of the other women looked remotely like a novelist. But then did she? It was always hard for her to assess her own appearance.

"It's mainly the hair," he said, answering her unspoken question. "So few women have long hair these days. Yours is beautiful."

"I don't write with my hair," she teased.

"Oh, no, I didn't—I was about to say—" He stammered and blushed.

She noticed his pronunciation of "about"—as if it rhymed with "throat" or "note"—and said in a gentler tone, "Are you Canadian?"

"Yes." He blushed again. "How did you know?"

"Those words: about, out, without." She tried to imitate the vowel, but couldn't get it quite right.

"Oh, yes—the shibboleths. They always make Americans laugh."

"I think they sound great." She found herself warming to him, despite his extreme good looks, which he in any case seemed unaware of. He doesn't act like a handsome man, she found herself thinking approvingly.

"Did you know the word *shibboleth* was itself used as a shibboleth?" she asked. "They could tell enemies from friends by the way it was pronounced, with a *shshsh* or a *sss*."

"I thought it was shibbole*th* or shibbole*t*," he said. "But it doesn't matter. What did it mean then, do you know?"

"I don't. Maybe just 'password.'" She took a sip of her soup, then added, "Although that would be hard to work into a casual conversation."

He laughed, loudly enough to attract a sudden glance from his wife, to whom he responded with a reassuring smile.

"How long have you been married?" Sarah asked him.

He rested his ringless left hand on the table, as if to contradict her. "How do you know I *am* married?"

Sarah shrugged. "The domestic nature of your expression when you smiled at her. The intimacy of it. I could be wrong."

"But you're not. Excellent powers of observation. You should be writing fiction."

At this they both laughed.

"And what do you do?" she asked.

"Well, I was trained as a lawyer. And then I spent a short time trying to be a writer myself. Didn't try hard enough, I guess, because nothing came of it. And now I help my wife with her work."

"Which is?"

"Writing a book. Not the kind of book *you* write; I guess you can't give anyone help with a novel. It's a nonfiction book—about war widows."

"You mean a history book? Or is it sociology?"

"Neither, really, although you could call it a little of both. It's more of a personal book. She's interviewing women whose husbands died in the Second World War, and using their voices as the text. And we think there will be photographs, too."

"Is she British?"

"French. We met in Canada, when she was over there interviewing—you know, a lot of Canadians died in the French battlefields. And then I just came back to Europe with her, and now we're doing the British interviews."

"How did she get interested in the subject?" Sarah glanced down the table at this woman about whom she had formed so many mistaken preconceptions.

Now it was his turn to pause over a spoonful of soup. "Her first husband," he said, wiping his mouth with the cloth napkin, "died in the war."

"Oh!" Sarah cried out, as if someone had stuck a pin in her. "Oh, how sad! Did they have any children?"

"No, no children. But she loved him very much. They had been childhood sweethearts, you see, and then her parents separated them by sending her off to a convent school. And then she went to university and he didn't. But afterwards they met again. By then he had become a film director, and when she married him she became his assistant. When the war broke out, he was offered a safe job making propaganda films for the Allies, and she pleaded with him to take it. But he said he had to fight, just like everyone else. So he joined the army. But he was no good at that sort of thing—he'd never fired a gun in his life, and he wasn't very strong. She knew when he left that she'd never see him again. He was killed in the first year."

Tears came to his eyes, and hers brimmed in response. This is ridiculous, she thought. I'm weeping because *he's* weeping for a man he never knew. His rival, even, though he probably doesn't think of it that way. She looked again at the French widow. If she had been married before the war, she must be a few years older than Sarah herself. Say, thirty-nine or forty at the very least. Whereas he—well, he must be more than a decade younger than his wife. Sarah wondered if the French woman minded. *She* would certainly mind. What right did anyone have to look so young?

"Are *you* married?" he asked. By now the soup course had been cleared, replaced by a plate containing brown slices of meat, olive-green florettes of broccoli, and potatoes in some kind of cream sauce.

"Divorced."

"Any children?"

"Two girls, six and nine." She looked up at him and continued as if defending herself: "They're home with a sitter."

"I'd love to meet them sometime." He answered her unconcealed look of surprise with an explanation that didn't really explain. "I love children."

Well, yes, she thought, that's all very well, but you hardly know me. Can you really, on half a meal's acquaintance, be inviting yourself over to my house? Or do you mean you hope you run into us on the street sometime? Or do you not mean anything at all?

This young man, Sarah decided, had insufficient social restraints. That, indeed, was part of what made him seem so young. It wasn't just his appearance. It was the way he came out with whatever he was thinking, as a child would, without calculating in advance the appropriateness of his remarks. His unguardedness was rather endearing, really, if a little strange.

And what about that story of the wife's first husband? To be spending his own life catering to her obsession about this lost love—for that's really what the book project came down to, if you took a firm view—well, that was very odd behavior for a handsome young man. One valued a sympathetic nature, of course, but this seemed excessive, as if he had given his whole self over to sympathy and retained nothing of his own. On the other hand, he wasn't boring, so he must have retained *something* . . .

She realized, belatedly, that he had asked her a question. "Sorry, what did you say?"

"I said, why did you get divorced? Were you unhappily married?"

"I used to say," she began, "that there was no such thing as happily or unhappily married. If you were unhappy, you got divorced. And if you were happy, that only lasted a couple of years anyway, after which you settled into domestic routine. When other women would complain to me about being bored, or restricted, or insufficiently in love with their husbands, I'd say, 'You are not unhappily married, you're just married.'"

She paused, but he continued to look at her with the same serious, inquiring expression.

"Most men find that remark funny. I see you don't. My husband—my ex-husband, I should say—never did either."

"But you haven't—"

"He left me for another woman," Sarah said brusquely.

"I'm sorry."

"Don't be. It's not your fault."

"I didn't mean it that way. I meant—I guess I meant to apologize for intruding, and also to say I don't understand how any man could want to leave you."

"You're very sweet." She touched the sleeve of his jacket slightly. "But you're very young."

"I can't be all that much younger than you are."

She waved her hand, not wanting to get into precisely those details. "That's not what I meant. You have a kind of child-like openness—a kind of idealism, or romanticism, I guess you'd say—that most people lose after the age of eighteen."

"Thank you. That sounds like a good way to be."

"It's very endearing, and it makes you very unusual. But it's not very practical."

"No. My wife is the practical one." He looked up the table again, where his wife appeared to be deeply engaged in conversation with their host.

"And does she shield you from reality? Is that how you've remained so unprotected?"

"Well, she's not my mother!" he laughed.

"You're right, it must have happened much earlier. Something in your childhood. Are you an only child?"

"No, I have an older sister."

"Well, what was it, do you think?"

He was silent a moment as their hostess came around to clear the dinner plates.

"I was very unattractive for a long time," he finally said. "Gawky, and awkward, and ugly. Or so I thought, and so everyone else made me feel. I didn't have any friends until I was about seventeen, and no girlfriends until I was nearly twenty. I spent a lot of time by myself. That's probably why I wanted to be a writer. I have a great respect for solitude, and a long acquaintance with it. I guess that's why I'm attracted to creative people, like my wife. Or like you."

She ignored his last remark. "But do you know now how attractive you are?"

"So I've been told," he smiled. "And I can look at myself and see things have improved since my teens. Well, some days—other days, you look in the mirror and see Nosferatu. But that's not the issue. The point is that your self-image is shaped at a much earlier stage, and it never much alters, does it? Even if you do. You know, they say that John Maynard Keynes felt inferior all his life because he'd been so unattractive as an adolescent. All that later success couldn't alter how he felt about himself."

"And do you think you're like John Maynard Keynes?"

"Oh, no, I wasn't—" He blushed again, furiously this time. "You must think I'm an egomaniac."

"No." Sarah patted his hand once, softly. "I think you're very sweet. And part of your sweetness is that you can't tell when I'm teasing you."

She faced away from him then and, for the rest of the dinner, talked generally with the other people at her end of the table. It wouldn't do to be gossiped about in these small-town circles, and she had already spent too much of the evening in a highly visible tête-à-tête. So it wasn't until they met in the front hallway, putting on their coats, that she again spoke to him.

"You know, I never learned your name."

"Tim. Tim West." He put out his hand, as if someone had only just introduced them.

She took it, laughing, and as she shook it, he leaned over and kissed her cheek.

"Good night," he said.

"Good night," she answered, and turned away quickly to hide the fact that this time it was she who was blushing.

HE RANG HER up two days later. "I have to go to London tomorrow, to deliver a package for my wife. Can I talk you into going with me? We could take the train and make a day of it. Museums, public gardens, that sort of thing."

"But the children—"

"Aren't they in school?"

"Well, yes, but only until four o'clock."

"Fine," he said. "I'll have you back before then. Can you meet me at the station at nine?"

"Yes," she said.

Sarah was both surprised and not surprised that he had called her. He was, she decided, unpredictable and therefore unreliable, given to extravagant speeches and gestures which he had no intention of following up on. This was not because he had a malicious nature, but because he didn't understand that his warm expressions of feeling implied any need for follow-up. Or perhaps the need for follow-up was her own peculiarity, and it was he who was normal. Either way, she had found herself thinking constantly about him ever since the dinner party.

She had begun by ringing up her friend Joan, her closest friend in England and her advisor about all local matters. Joan had been in Cambridge so long she even sounded English, at least to Sarah's ear, though she had actually come from Australia as a student. Jack, Sarah's ex-husband, had never taken to Joan. "I'm sure she's a dyke," Jack always said. "She can't stand men. I can tell."

"Oh, don't be ridiculous," Sarah would respond. "Just because she doesn't like *you* . . . I happen to know she has a new boyfriend every two minutes." Secretly, she felt, Jack really wanted Joan to be a lesbian so he could imagine them doing sexily forbidden things to each other in his absence. Men seemed to enjoy indulging in such fantasies. Far harder for them to imagine that women might simply want to *talk* to somebody, for a change.

"He's very attractive," she confided to her friend the morning after the dinner party. Sarah was sitting at her desk, where she usually sat when they carried on these near-daily phone calls. She could imagine Joan leaning against the counter in her kitchen, where the flat's sole phone hung on the wall. She would be dressed already for her lectures and supervisions.

Sarah sometimes envied her these daily outings into the world of the university, this routine imposed by others.

"Younger, I suppose," said Joan drily.

"Much."

"How much?"

"I don't know. I didn't want to ask, for fear I'd have to tell."

"Jesus, Sarah, thirty-six isn't *that* old."

"It is if you're twenty-six."

"That bad, eh?"

"Something like that."

"I don't know why you always find callowness so attractive."

"It's not the callowness I like. It's the romanticism. Anyway, it may all come to nothing. I can't even tell if he's interested in me."

"Not to mention the fact that there's a wife."

"Yes, well, but she's French, and doesn't seem to care much. Or maybe she has him on such a tight leash, emotionally, that she doesn't have to care. He does seem more involved in her life than she is in his."

"Isn't it the same life, with married people?"

"It never was in my case," Sarah said.

"I suppose you flirted madly with this boy."

"What do you mean? You know I never flirt."

"That's what I mean. Sometimes not flirting can be the most compelling form of flirtation."

Now, dressing to meet Tim at the train station, Sarah tried to analyze what she was expecting. Did she really want to have a love affair? Did she really imagine that was possible? She examined her body in the full-length mirror that hung on the door of the wardrobe. The belly was a bit pouchy from two children, and the breasts had begun to droop. The legs were still in pretty good shape, but her legs had never been her best feature because they were too short. She still had a waist, and her wide shoulders emphasized it. Her face wasn't too bad either, though the little lines were beginning to be noticeable, especially around the eyes. Neither the face nor the body would launch a thousand ships, she thought. Still, people had their own weird preferences, and you could never be sure what would attract someone.

"I'm so glad you could come!" Tim said, throwing his arm around her and hurrying her out onto the platform. "It will be a great adventure."

Facing her in the carriage (he had volunteered to ride backward, which she thought was immensely chivalrous), he asked her, "What did your husband do?"

"He was—is, I should say—a screenwriter."

"How funny that my wife's husband and your husband should both be in films."

"Ex-husband," Sarah reminded him. "Yes, but very different kinds of films, I'm sure. He was quite the Hollywood success story, until his Communist past caught up with him. It was the McCarthy era that drove us over here in the first place. He couldn't get work in America any more."

"But why Cambridge? It hardly seems a major film center."

"Oh, that was just part of his slimy plot. He parked me and the kids out in Cambridge and went into London every day to work. Gradually it turned out that he needed to stay over two or three nights a week to keep an eye on things and—well, you can see where that led."

"Is he still over here?"

"No, he went back last year."

"Why did you stay, then?"

"Inertia, I guess. England is a good country for a writer. You can feel as if the written word still matters here. And the girls were settled in school, and they had their friends. And I suppose I had my friends, too, and the house, and the garden. I'm not close to my family, and I've never felt very patriotic about America. Really, I feel much more American here than I ever did at home. So I just stayed. But you never know—I might go back someday."

"I think about going back a lot," he said. "France is a difficult place for a Canadian. They laugh at my accent, and my French was never really very good anyway. If I could talk my wife into it, we'd live over here instead, as a kind of compromise location. But she can't stand the English, though she pretends to tolerate them. I think, obscurely, she blames them for her husband's death—as if they didn't do enough soon enough to squelch Hitler."

"Nobody did," Sarah pointed out.

"No, that's true."

"How long will you be here, then?"

"Oh, a few more weeks, I would guess. I never know. It depends on how quickly Marie-Claire gets her work done."

From King's Cross they took a taxi to the heart of Bloomsbury, where he accomplished his errand by leaving a parcel at an imposing building in Queen's Square.

"Where to now?" he said. "Greenwich? Kew Gardens? The British Museum?"

She chose the nearby museum, thinking that it would be fun to take him through the Elgin Marbles. Sarah had seen them only once herself, and she looked forward to renewing the acquaintance. But when they arrived in the temporary galleries where the sculptures were housed ("Temporary since the Second World War," Sarah scoffed, implying that only the English could be guilty of such a delay), she found that the friezes from the Parthenon now looked entirely different to her, as if they were new and not familiar works of art. Three years earlier, when she had first seen them, they seemed to represent the pinnacle of high art, form for form's sake alone. Now, however, she could only think about how much the Greek sculptors had loved the unclothed male body. The artistic had become the erotic, and the tribute to the gods was now a tribute to boyish manhood.

"I like these best." Tim pointed to panels containing individual centaurs that struggled, in various degrees of fragmentation, with individual men.

"Yes," she agreed, standing before one in which the man seemed to have the bearded centaur in some kind of stranglehold. "They're very powerful, very strongly felt."

"Very modern," he added. "You can see what Michelangelo was aspiring to." He sighed. "The depressing thing about looking at works like these is you feel it's downhill all the way from there."

"True, but it's no reason not to keep chipping away at one's own little block of marble. If I tried to compete with the great novelists I love most, I'd never write a word."

"I think that's a view only a woman could hold. Men are more ambitious. We need to compete with the past."

"Is that why you had to quit writing?"

"Touché," Tim laughed, and took her by the hand to lead her along to the next frieze.

"I have an idea," Sarah said when they had covered all three galleries. "Let's go to Sir John Soane's museum."

"What's that?"

"You'll see."

It was cold but not raining, so they walked down Southampton Row and Kingsway, turning left into Lincoln's Inn Fields. She was relieved to find the museum open, since she was never sure of its hours. They checked their heavy coats at the front and began to move through the artifact-engorged rooms.

"Bit of a monstrosity, isn't it?" Tim murmured in her ear. There wasn't another soul in the place, but something in the atmosphere made them want to lower their voices.

"Wait," she whispered back. "It earns its keep in here."

She took him into the small paneled room that lay toward the back of the museum's first floor, just to the right of a basement alcove housing a Roman sarcophagus. As the wooden shutters on the walls swung back, revealing each painting in the sequence, Tim audibly caught his breath. "*The Rake's Progress*? It's *here*?"

Sarah nodded, proud to have presented him with this rare gift. She turned to the picture just beside her, *The Orgy*, with its pox-faced, half-dressed young women surrounding the lolling young Rake. From this she moved along to her favorite in the series, the final scene set in Bedlam, where the Rake, naked except for a loin cloth, lay like a Pietà Christ in the lap of his abandoned mistress. As she gazed at the odd, unnerving picture, she could feel Tim standing behind her, looking at it as well. And then she felt his hands around both her shoulders. She turned to him inquiringly, her face lifted, and he kissed her briefly on the lips.

They had no sooner broken apart when a harsh female voice rang out. "Sarah? Sarah Jameson? What on earth are you doing here?"

Sarah whipped around to face Ida Lingman, wife of the red-faced Herb, who had just appeared in the doorway of the little room. Or *had* she just appeared? There was no way to know how much she had seen.

"Ida!" Sarah stammered. "Uh, I could ask the same of you." She tried to soften her startled tone with a smile.

"I'm giving my sister-in-law the London tour. I don't think you've met Herb's sister. She just arrived yesterday. Alice?" she called, a little too loudly. "Come meet a friend of mine from Cambridge. This is Sarah Jameson—the novelist, you know." A rather pale, shrunken, greyish-blonde-haired lady, the physical antonym of Herb Lingman, took Sarah's hand. "And this—" Ida paused tellingly.

"Oh, I'm sorry. I thought you had met the other night," Sarah apologized. "This is Tim West."

"Pleased to meet you," said Tim, shaking each of the older women by the hand and conferring on each in turn his dazzling smile.

"Did you two know each other from the States?" Ida asked.

"Oh, no." Sarah tried to answer airily, but she felt a mild tone of hysteria entering her voice. "Tim's Canadian, not American. You'd know if he said one of the words."

Ida gave her an odd look.

"We just met at the Gardners' the other night," Tim explained. "And since my wife and I have only recently come to Britain, and my wife had to work today, Sarah kindly offered to give me the London museum tour."

Sarah gave him a slightly indignant look—who had invited whom, after all?—but he answered her with a look that said, Trust me to handle this one. And, uncharacteristically, she did.

"Oh, how nice," Ida said, as if she didn't really think it was very nice at all. "Would you two like to join us for lunch?"

"Well, you see—" Sarah began.

"I'm afraid we can't," Tim interrupted, frowning charmingly. "I promised to get Sarah back to Cambridge in time to pick up her children from school, and that means we haven't time. It's too bad, isn't it? It would have been a perfect way to round out the tour." He turned to Sarah for confirmation, and she nodded—like a ventriloquist's dummy, she thought.

"Oh, well, another time," smiled Ida.

"Yes, indeed," said Tim.

When they had safely escaped the building, Sarah turned to him. "Do you have to charm everybody?"

"What do you mean?"

"Well, it's like this tap that you just turn on. A woman comes into view and—whoosh!—out pours the charm."

He looked hurt. "I don't mean to be hypocritical or dishonest. That's just the way I am. I don't see any point in not being nice to people."

"No, you wouldn't," she said. "You need more hate in you."

"I *need* it? What do you mean? To be a better person?"

"No." She reached up and stroked his cheek. "You're a perfectly good person as you are, and I'm not trying to change your character. I just mean that if you had more hate in you, you wouldn't be so open and vulnerable. But then, that's a large part of the appeal."

Back in Cambridge, he insisted on going with her to pick up the children. The two girls were shy and mistrustful at first. (Sarah rarely brought home strange men, and when she did her daughters always made their disapproval apparent.) But Tim's childlike way of telling stories and jokes soon won them over. The older girl animatedly recounted to him the gist of the day's lesson in Greek mythology.

"I like the Greek gods best," she confided, "because they have little flaws. It's hard to like a perfect god."

He laughed and praised her for her wisdom. A bit later, when the girls had left them alone in Sarah's kitchen, he repeated the praise to Sarah. "Very bright girls," he told her. "And very nice."

"Thank you. I think so too." She paused a moment. "I worry though, sometimes, that they're growing up English. They don't even *sound* American any more."

"Well, and what's wrong with that? I thought you liked living here."

"I do, but I had a chance to be formed elsewhere. It's being American in England that I like. I don't want my girls turning into straightforward Englishwomen. I don't even like English-women, for the most part."

"Ah, now you sound like my wife!"

As he left he took her hand but didn't kiss her. "See you soon," he said, and was out the door before she could even reply.

"I CAN'T FIGURE him out," she told Joan the next morning on the telephone. "Sometimes he seems interested in me, and sometimes not. He goes hot and cold, and I can't keep up."

"Maybe he's just an aspiring writer seeking an entrée into the literary world."

"Thanks a lot. Trust you to come up with the explanation that's least flattering to my vanity."

"Oh, I don't know about that. I think the fact that you're a novelist—a good, respected novelist—is rather central to your personality."

"It wasn't my personality I was hoping he was interested in."

Joan changed tack. "What does he look like?"

"Oh, you know, my usual type. Dark hair, dark eyes, strong features, rather thin face."

"With a name like Tim West? What is he, Black Irish?"

"No, half-Italian. At least, he said his mother was Italian." Sarah's tone conveyed an element of doubt.

"It's not the sort of thing one would make up," remarked Joan.

"No, it's not," Sarah agreed, realizing that her doubt stemmed from other causes. It wasn't his factual statements she doubted, but the intentions behind them—or perhaps what she doubted was the very existence of such intentions.

When she got off the phone she found that she was unusually restless, unable to begin on her morning's work. Damn it, Sarah thought, a pleasant distraction is one thing, but when it begins to interfere with my writing . . . The problem was that she couldn't very well achieve peace of mind by resolving to get rid of him when she didn't even have him. Yet. Or possibly ever. That indecidability, she decided, was what made the distraction so distracting.

She killed twenty minutes by brewing up a pot of tea, then returned to her desk with a milky cup of Twining's English Breakfast. But even after she had drained the cup—and another after that—she found that the unfinished story resisted her. She held her pen firmly, but it refused to give anything up to the paper; it refused even to meet the white surface of the blank page. Annoyed at her inanimate materials, and even more annoyed at herself, she threw down the pen and went to have a pee.

There, in the dank, grey closet that housed the weirdly antiquated toilet fixture, she discovered that her period had unexpectedly started a day or two early. Sarah cursed aloud. She stuffed a wad of the slick, beige, insufficiently absorbent toilet paper between her legs and, with her pants still down around her ankles, hobbled into the bath cubicle next door.

From the medicine chest she retrieved her elastic belt, and from the built-in cupboard by the sink she took one of the pads from the box of Kotex she regularly had shipped from America. She had found the English version of sanitary pads intolerable. And I could do with a real, American-style bathroom too, she fumed to herself, removing the bloody toilet paper from between her thighs and temporarily leaving it in the sink as she struggled to pull the pad's paper ends through the straps without getting blood all over the bathroom floor. Thank God Jack wasn't here to complain. Her periods always seemed to irritate him unreasonably, especially after they had moved to England. It wasn't as if she tried to leave blood all over the house, for Christ's sake. It was just that if you had the toilet in one place and all the rest of the bathroom equipment somewhere else— Sarah stopped herself in mid-argument, plucked the soiled paper from the sink, did a quick rinse from the cold faucet, and went back next door to the toilet. As she pulled the chain to flush away the bloody evidence, she was aware of the familiar discomfort of the pad between her legs, like a wearisome fuzzing of her physical sensations, a perceptible gag on her normally unconscious grace of movement. The day was evidently destined to be a dead loss. She would forget about writing and instead work in the garden. It was remarkably sunny for the first of November—a good day to put the garden to bed for the winter.

She was out by the front gate, squatting to pick up the thorny branches she had just clipped from the iceberg rose, when she heard an unfamiliar voice say, "Hello." The voice had some kind of accent, neither English nor American, and when Sarah shook her hair back and looked up over the low fence, she saw she was being greeted by Tim's wife.

"Oh! Hello!" What the hell was her name? "Marie-Claire, isn't it?" She stood up and brushed her dirty hands against her ratty old pedal pushers, then held out her right hand with a slightly apologetic expression. "Sorry about the dirt. I'm Sarah Jameson."

"I know," said the Frenchwoman, taking Sarah's hand in both of hers and looking directly into her eyes. "You have been so very kind to my husband. He has told me how you showed him the lovely museums of London yesterday. I am so grateful, because when I have to work he can easily get bored— except when he is helping me, of course, but he cannot be helping me every minute." Marie-Claire smiled in what Sarah considered an inscrutable fashion. Then she released her hand.

Sarah felt as if there was something wrong with her reaction time. Her hand seemed to float a moment too long over the fence before she pulled it back to her side, and her voice was correspondingly slow in emerging from her throat. "Oh—" To her own ears it sounded like a croak, so she gave a slight cough and began again. "Oh, is he a big help to you?"

"Oh, yes, very big. But of course these boys who did not fight in the war themselves, they are too inexperienced, they cannot understand. But he is so sympathetic, so nice to the war widows, that they do not perceive this. They think he understands, and that is what matters, for it brings out their confessions."

Sarah wondered fleetingly if "sympathetic" was really what she meant. Didn't *sympathique* have some other connotation?

She tossed her head slightly as if to brush away this buzzingly intrusive thought.

"I didn't realize," she told the older woman, "that you did the interviews together."

"Oh, yes," nodded Marie-Claire. "I ask the questions and Tim runs the apparatus. The—how do you call it?—the tape machine. He is my 'sound man.' Is that right?"

"Yes, sound man. Like in the movies."

"The movies, yes. You have worked in the movies?"

"No, but my husband did."

Marie-Claire's face suddenly took on a look of intense, collegial sadness. "Your husband is dead?"

"No," Sarah laughed. "Just living in America, with another woman." And then, to undo the look of prim embarrassment that came over the other woman's face, she added: "Don't worry. I don't mind talking about the divorce. Some husbands are better absent than present."

"I have not found this," Marie-Claire replied seriously. "A husband is a very important thing."

"Well, perhaps you've just been luckier in your choice of husbands than I have." Almost immediately, Sarah regretted her cavalier tone. But it was too late to do anything about it, and in any case she didn't much care. As they moved away from the fence, each on the opposite side, she raised her hand in a silent wave, a gesture that coincided exactly with the Frenchwoman's hurriedly whispered "*Au revoir*, Mrs. Jameson."

That night the girls were particularly loving when she tucked them into bed. Loving, or about to come down with something? She could never be sure, when they got cuddly and affectionate, whether it was due to an impending fever, a recent anxiety, or just a new development in their ever-changing personalities. It was so sweet, in any case, that she hesitated to investigate the sources.

"When is Daddy coming home?" murmured the six-year-old as she drifted close to sleep. Sarah was startled but not shocked, having already explained the divorce at least half a dozen times.

She remained silent a moment, stunned by the pain she was once again about to inflict. "He's not coming home to live here, darling," she said. "You know that. But he loves you very much, and he misses you, and he's going to have you come stay with him for a long time in the summer."

"How far away is the summer?"

Sarah smiled. "Still pretty far."

"I'm afraid I'm forgetting," said the little girl.

"Forgetting what, hon?"

"What he was like. What it was like to have him here. I can feel myself forgetting."

Sarah bit her lip and looked over at her older daughter, who was lying in bed like an Egyptian mummy, her face coldly impassive, her open eyes focused on the ceiling. She was pretending not to have heard, wearing her guise of utter detachment, as if none of this embarrassingly explicit sentiment had anything to do with her. I should be grateful, Sarah thought, that at least one of them is still capable of expressing sorrow. But it was not much of a consolation.

SHE DIDN'T SEE Tim again until the Maxwells' election-night party. To say this gathering had become a tradition in the Cambridge expatriate community would be to exaggerate its antiquity. The first one had occurred in 1952, when the Maxwells and most of their guests had only recently arrived in England; this one was therefore just the second. In between there had been annual Guy Fawkes Day parties—to hold the place, as it were—but none of the Americans could get very worked up at this strange British rite, a cross between the Fourth of July and Halloween, with a bit of a football-season bonfire thrown in. They much preferred the chance to hash over their own distant local politics.

As the Maxwells elaborately acknowledged on their invitation cards, a real American election-night party would always be held on a Tuesday. But since the results of the voting wouldn't be known in Britain by Tuesday night—since, in fact, the polls in America wouldn't even be closed until after midnight Greenwich time—the party was set for the evening of Wednesday the 7th. By the time Sarah joined the festivities, she had long since heard the discouraging results.

At any other party held in Cambridge that night, political discussion would have been dominated by Suez, or possibly Hungary, but here at the Maxwells' it was all about the American election. By bad luck, the first person Sarah ran across as she entered the crowded front room was Herb Lingman, already well into his cups, his face blazing like a stoplight. He clapped her heartily on the shoulder and then kept his heavy hand resting there, leaning over her slightly as if he were an avuncular schoolmaster about to convey an important kernel of wisdom to a bright but rebellious pupil.

"Well, my dear, you see I was right after all. The country has gone for Ike."

"Your side won," Sarah answered, somewhat testily. "That doesn't mean you were right."

"You can't seriously have thought that egg-head ever had a chance with the American people."

"Egg-head!" sputtered Sarah. "I hate that word. Anyway, Eisenhower's the one that *looks* like an egg. Soft-boiled, if you ask me, so the babyish palates of the American public can suck him down easily."

"Whoa, you're certainly a sore loser! But definitely in the minority. I'm sure most of our countrymen would agree with me in calling our President quite a *good egg*." Herb delivered his bon mot with such audible italics, such evident pleasure in his own wit, that Sarah could only roll her eyes in response. She eased out from under the schoolmasterly clutch and headed toward the drinks table.

With a tall gin-and-tonic in hand (on ice, she was relieved to see, since the hosts served their drinks American-style), she positioned herself in the corner of the room and surveyed the gathering. Sarah was rare among her acquaintances in that she not only enjoyed cocktail parties but openly admitted to enjoying them. At a dinner party, she had been known to point out, you were stuck at the table, surrounded by the two or three people your hostess had decided you should get to know, whereas a cocktail party left you free to roam. If someone got boring or pushy or otherwise disagreeable, you merely had to go freshen your drink. When she talked this way, Sarah's friends all said, yes, but didn't she find that the social encounters one had at cocktail parties were so *superficial*. "But that's the beauty of them," Sarah would answer. "They're short and fast, and that offers certain opportunities for wit or sharpness or intensity. You can present yourself in heightened form, in a way that's not possible or appropriate in a longer conversation. If you're going to enjoy these things, you have to like the abbreviated format. Think of it as a sonnet rather than an epic poem."

And now, from her corner, she at last spotted the Wests. Tim and Marie-Claire had just, apparently, come in, so recently that they were still standing together, in that stranded way married couples do before they've had time to be absorbed into the swirl of a large party. Soon, however, they drifted apart in the crowd. Sarah kept her eye on the handsome young man—*her* handsome young man, as she thought of him—while he stood talking with an equally attractive, and equally young, woman. Who was that girl, anyway? A research student of Fred Maxwell's? A friend of the Lingmans' university-age daughter? No matter. The point was her youth. It shone from her face and brought out all Tim's boyishness in response, as if in a reflected glow.

Sarah felt herself beginning to seethe with an unbecoming, inappropriate, and completely irresistible feeling of jealousy. Who did he think he was? Why was he ignoring her so publicly, and instead paying so much attention to this blonde dimwit? (Sarah admittedly knew nothing of the girl's intellectual achievements or lack thereof, but she wasn't about to allow accuracy to interfere with the solace of insulting thoughts.) Did other people notice how well-matched the two of them seemed? Did they think it was nice he had finally found someone his own age? And (here jealousy was joined by humiliation) did they lump her in with Marie-Claire as one of the middle-aged hags who had previously tried to monopolize him? She had been a fool to think this charming kid could ever be interested in her.

Charming? Who said he was charming? Joan had, after all, called him callow. But then, Sarah reminded herself, Joan had never met him. She had just assumed he was callow because he was young. Well, and was he? Sarah tried to recall the exact words of their conversations, the look in his eye as he'd spoken to her or listened to her speak. No, he wasn't stupid, not by any means. Still, there was something slightly off-kilter about him. He lacked something men her age mostly had. (American men, at any rate; she couldn't speak with authority about Canadians.) And what was that something? She struggled to come up with it. A sense of their own weightiness? An undertone of aggression? Menace? That's what it was. He utterly lacked menace.

Having reached this thought, Sarah smiled slightly to herself, and at exactly that moment Tim happened to catch her eye. He grinned broadly and raised his glass to her. Unsmiling now, she lifted hers in response, then noticed it was empty.

She had no idea how many gin-and-tonics had gone by when Fred at last pulled out his guitar. Sooner or later every Maxwell party reached this point, and guests who had been coming for years knew how to time their departures to the warning signs. Enough people always remained, however, out of politeness or inertia or even (though this seemed unlikely) an actual desire to hear Fred play, to offer their host the sense of a festive audience. Apparently Fred had recently discovered Argentinian tango music. That, at least, was what he seemed to be imitating, in a manner that certainly made up in wholeheartedness what it lacked in technique.

The music, or Fred's execution of it, was bringing smiles to people's faces; either way, the party had acquired a new overtone of jollity. Sarah found herself reflexively grinning, and suddenly she noticed that Tim was by her side. She gave him a conspiratorial glance, a have-you-ever-heard-such-incompetent-guitar-playing sort of look. But he, to her surprise, was not smiling. He had a glassy, intent look on his face. (Perhaps, she realized belatedly, he was drunk. Having never seen him drunk before, she had no idea how it would strike him.) He opened his arms toward her, in a courtly imitation of a tango dancer's welcoming embrace. She smiled hesitantly, as if to acknowledge the jest. Then he closed his arms around her and began to propel her across the room.

Sarah's first impulse was to break from his arms and flee. But everyone was looking at them and beaming. Everyone thought it was a good joke. Fred even began to make some kind of silly yipping sound, as if to accompany the dancers in authentic fashion. Resignation, she decided, was therefore the better part of valor. She would just have to get through the dance. But *could* she dance? And—perhaps more to the point, since he was leading—could *he*?

Tim reached the far side of the widening gap that was being allotted to them in the Maxwells' none-too-spacious front room and abruptly swung her about, changing his grip as he did so. He started to tilt her off her feet into a low swoop, and she felt herself stiffen. *I look like a fool* and *He's going to drop me* were the thoughts simultaneously running through her mind. He put his face close to hers. "Trust me!" he hissed in her ear. "You have to trust me!"

It was not in her nature to do this on command. But even she, greatly as she believed in resisting the tide, saw that things would go more smoothly if for once she allowed herself to be swept along. So she relaxed into his arms and tried to match her stride to his long, low, potentially ridiculous gait. She felt as if they were skimming across the floor at about a hundred miles an hour. Each time they made one of their extravagant turns, the audience whooped and clapped with approval. Sarah started to laugh. She was, she realized, enjoying herself. Tim, however, continued to look very serious, as if the dance were an assignment he needed to fulfill perfectly in order to complete his share in a collaborative work of art.

At last Fred stopped playing—luckily, or coincidentally, on the end of a phrase. In the roar of drunken applause that met their final downward swoop, Tim held Sarah a moment longer than was strictly necessary. Then, having righted her, he stepped back, lifted her hand, and kissed it with a low bow. Sarah instinctively curtseyed deeply (a holdover, perhaps, from years of childhood dance classes), and when she looked up again, he had disappeared into the crowd.

SHE NEVER SAW him again. In a week he had gone, leaving with Marie-Claire for the next stop in their interviewing tour. Why this should rankle so with her—why she should spend countless hours, while the children were at school, thinking back on their few encounters—was not a problem she was capable of resolving. This obsession seemed so silly that she couldn't even mention it to Joan. Was it her heart that was wounded, or just her vanity? He had, after all, promised her nothing. But she felt his sudden departure as a broken promise nonetheless. What had she been hoping for? A quick fling? A serious love affair? A whole new life? She felt ridiculous, and old. She should be past such adolescent imaginings and hopes. She knew the score. She had had her innings.

Where in the world did these sports metaphors come from? It was as if she were seeing things through Jack's mind. This was *his* kind of language. And *he* was the one who thought she was too old. That wasn't an objective truth; thirty-six wasn't old. In fact, it was younger than Jack, and *he* was still out there batting away. But having reached this point, Sarah sighed to herself. Objectivity meant nothing. It was all in the perceptions. And the perceptions of men were different. Compared to a thirty-six-year-old man, she was old.

"Oh, don't be ridiculous," Joan snapped, when Sarah remarked on this fact as they were preparing Thanksgiving dinner. Doing Thanksgiving for the natives had been Sarah's idea, and Joan had eagerly offered to help. Sarah's plan was to invite only their British and European—and, as Joan reminded her, Australian—friends; it would be a novelty, for the guests and for the hostess. And it would be a relief, for once, to break out of the tight little world of the American expatriate community. The only Americans present, as she envisioned it, would be herself and her daughters—but the girls, who considered themselves completely English by now, had thought the whole thing sounded boring, so Sarah sent them off to spend the night with a neighboring family.

"I'm not being ridiculous, I'm being realistic." Sarah opened the oven door and eyed the turkey with evident mistrust. "How long do you think this thing needs to cook?"

"Hours and hours, I should think. Especially if you're going to keep opening the oven door." Joan peered over her shoulder. "It looks awfully pale to me."

"Maybe we should turn the heat up."

"What does it say in the cookbook?"

"I don't use cookbooks," Sarah announced. "I usually just ask people."

"Well, did you ask one of the Americans about roasting a turkey?"

"No, I couldn't, since none of them were invited." She gave a slightly hysterical laugh. "Did you set the table yet?"

"Yes, but I couldn't find serviettes."

"Oh, my God—I forgot to buy them, and it's too late now. All the shops will be closed."

"Well, do you have cloth?"

"Are you kidding? In this household?" Sarah rummaged in a drawer by the sink and came up with a single crumpled paper napkin. "We'll just have to share this." At which point Joan too became hysterical.

It was not until they were putting together the salad, some time later, that Joan returned to the subject. "Anyway, age is relative. It depends who you're older than. Or do I mean whom? But speaking of which, I can't wait to tell you what I heard about your friend Tim West."

"Hardly my friend, since he didn't even call to say goodbye."

"I detect a touch of rancor there. But the point is, it turns out that my only Canadian friend, someone I hadn't heard from in a few years, *knows* him. It came up when my friend called last week. Isn't that amazing? Makes you think there are only a hundred people in the whole country. I had heard it was underpopulated, but—"

"Joan!" Sarah stopped the digressive flow in exasperation. "You're killing me with the suspense. What did your friend say?"

"Oh, sorry, dear. Well, he knew Tim from McGill, apparently—they were university chums. And he said there was something funny medically, some illness or propensity or whatever, that kept Tim out of the army, kept him from serving in the war."

"Serving in the war? What war?"

"What war? You idiot, the Second World War. What else could I be talking about? He's hardly old enough for the First."

"But I thought—I mean, I didn't think he was nearly old enough for the Second." Sarah did a quick calculation in her head. "If he was old enough to serve when they were calling people up in Canada . . . well, that means he's got to be over thirty at the very least."

"Thirty-five. He's the same age as my friend."

"But . . . but . . ." Sarah was sputtering—with surprise? with rage? she didn't know. "But he's practically my age. And the whole time I thought he was at least a decade younger."

"So? That's my point. Anyway, what difference does it make?"

Sarah couldn't answer her. For once, she was speechless. What difference *did* it make? That she had misread his age was hardly a stupid error—he looked ten years younger, at least. So she could hardly be blamed for her misperception. And there had been that utterly boyish manner. Was that the problem? Had the boyishness been the appeal, and had she now been robbed of that? No, he still had his appeal; she tested it in her mind, like a tongue reaching for a sore tooth, and found it still as much alive as ever. If anything, the problem was the very opposite. She had thought he was unavailable to her, finally, because of his age—that he had been toying with her as a younger man will toy, socially, gallantly, but finally unseriously, with a hopelessly older woman. Only now it turned out that she was barely older at all. He had merely been toying with her because—well, because he didn't want her enough to do more than toy.

Why do I get myself into these things? she wondered. Why do I allow myself to be hurt by someone I hardly know? Who is he to me, that he should have this kind of power over me? And at this a terrible feeling of shame washed over her. But whether it was shame at being undesired, or shame at wanting so much to be desired that she allowed even the most casual encounter to make her feel rejected, she never did succeed in figuring out.

In later years, when Sarah thought back on this period of her life, she found herself unable to reconstruct what had happened to her. She could remember the facts—that she had met this boy (or, rather, man), that she had seen him only a few times, that she had longed for him in an intense, raging, futile way. But she could not, from a later date, enter in any way into that obsession. She could not experience it as real. Even with her pen in her hand, trying to conjure him up, she could not make Tim West into something as substantial as one of her own fictional characters. His opacity resisted her. This was not just a problem of understanding or belief, but one of recollection. It was as if she had suffered from some kind of high fever that overwhelmed all her perceptions, dominated her life for a time, and then passed, as fevers will do, leaving her with only the vaguest memory of having once been ill.

Book Three
1973–1975

THE COLD WAS the first thing she noticed when she arrived in Cambridge—no, the second thing, after the beauty. She walked around, for the first few days, in a state of heightened attention, astonished by the grand design of the Chapel and the green dignity of the Backs and the wonderful view through the central arch in the eighteenth-century Gibbs building. It was all beautifully strange and at the same time oddly familiar.

"Like a fairy tale, almost," she said to her friend Adam, who, though he was assigned to one of the newer, outlying colleges, had kindly ventured into the city center to help her admire her own. She pointed at the Gibbs archway, through which neo-classical sheep could be distantly seen, placidly grazing. "Don't you feel you could just walk through that into the past?"

"No," he answered, characteristically deflating her characteristic excess. "I don't. And even if I did feel that, I'm not sure I'd want to. The past wasn't always such a delightful place to be."

"But at least it would be a change. A chance to lead a different kind of life."

"Not necessarily," he responded. "I think it's all just cyclical. You know what Marx said," he grinned.

"I know, I know. History repeats itself."

"You're leaving out the best part," he corrected her. "*The first time as tragedy, the second time as farce.*" She made a face at him—an *I*-knew-that grimace—and he gave her an I-*knew-you*-knew-that smile in return.

But however much Adam teased her, she couldn't escape her own sense of having wandered into a dream. She found an echo of her feeling in a story by her favorite writer, who had been transplanted from America to these parts a century before her. "The latent preparedness of the American mind even for the most characteristic features of English life," the expatriate novelist had written, "was a matter I meanwhile failed to get to the bottom of. The roots of it are so deeply buried in the soil of our early culture that, without some great upheaval of feeling, we are at a loss to say exactly when and where and how it begins. It makes an American's enjoyment of England more searching than anything Continental. I had seen the coffee-room of the Red Lion years ago, at home— at Saragossa, Illinois—in books, in visions, in dreams, in Dickens, in Smollett, in Boswell." Yes, she thought, as she copied the words into her journal (for she too had visions, had dreams). And then, book closed, she went back out on the Cambridge streets to wander and admire.

As she admired she shivered, for she had brought only the kinds of clothes that would be appropriate to a New York September. Her warm things were all coming later, by trunk. In the end she broke down and bought a garish purple sweater in the open market that daily occupied the square in front of the Cambridge Town Hall. It went oddly with her summer clothes, but she was at an age when she thought very little about how she looked to outsiders, and in any case there were no outsiders to scrutinize her with any but the most passing interest.

Until she met Paul. And even then she was less concerned with how she looked than how she sounded, since she was too young to believe that anything else mattered.

He would drop by her college room and, as he waited for her to make him a cup of tea, would casually take off his shoes. He always did this when he sat down, as if from a childhood habit of wearing shoes too big or too small, handed down from other feet, therefore uncomfortable to his. It was his one great informality. Otherwise he was classically English, despite his poor background and mild Cockney accent. He had the bad teeth and the slight build and the fair, easily reddened complexion and the soft, downy hair that she associated with his nation. There was something appealingly feminine about him, compared to any American man she knew. (That's why she disliked English women, she decided: they were *too* female, to the point of prissy affectation. The whole scale had been shifted over toward the feminine side in England.) And he in turn found her bracingly, amusingly American. She didn't know if she attracted him, but she was sure she intrigued him. Not having been to America at all, he found her unusual, one of a kind. She, on the other hand, was more interested in the ways they both represented the general.

"I like to see things as specific instances," he once said, in his scientist's manner, with two centuries of British empiricism behind him. "Whereas you tend to generalize wildly on the basis of two or three examples."

"Hm," she said. "I wonder if that's typical of Americans." And then she laughed at the despairing look he gave her.

One of the things she treasured about him was his psychological backwardness. He was intelligent, had read a fair amount, and could pick up on an interesting idea as soon as the next person. But he had never, it seemed, heard of Freud. Or rather, he had heard the name and let it pass, as the label of some turn-of-the-century crank whose Continental ideas had nothing to do with British character—that is, with reality. She found this charming, and remarkable, as if she were an anthropologist who had discovered a foreign culture that used, say, nuclear power and automobiles but had yet to invent the idea of God. To discover Paul's ignorance of Freud (if ignorance was the right word for such a willful, such an enormous cultural omission) was to encounter a whole new continent, a virgin land ripe for colonization. She proceeded to proselytize. He would tell her his dreams—narrating them with an innocent openness, an utter lack of repression or embarrassment—and she would say, "Yes, well . . ." He was fascinated, and she felt like a female Joseph in Egypt. His supply of dreams was endless, as were her interpretations, and it was the interpretations they both found so compelling.

But still he treated it as a parlor trick, as merely a funny game she could play with him, until one day they went to London to see a production of *Antony and Cleopatra* at the Aldwych. As they entered the Underground station on the last leg of their long journey by bus and train and now subway, he started to hand his yellow stub to the ticket collector at the beginning of their ride. The uniformed collector, with a smile, pushed the ticket back at him, and Paul smiled too at his silly mistake, for of course everyone knew that you handed in the tickets at the end of the ride, not at the beginning. He himself had been doing it for years.

"Well," he said, turning to her with his still-sheepish smile, though it was now beginning to shift into the ironic grin of one who knows he has won before the discussion even begins, "and what would Dr. Freud make of *that* little mistake, eh?" He was so confident that there could, in fact, be meaningless mistakes.

But she burst his balloon. "He would say that you wish you were at the end of the journey already—either because you're tired of traveling, or because you don't really want to go to this play, or whatever. But you wish you were coming out of the subway, rather than going in." And the look of shock on his face was the outer acknowledgment that he had been read correctly, even before he could read himself. After that he was no longer a skeptic.

They saw a great deal of each other. On Sundays, when the College didn't serve lunch, they would often go on a walk together, ending up at a pub where they could buy a cold meat pie and a half-pint of cider (in her case) and a ploughman's lunch and a pint of bitter (in his). Her favorite route was the walk to Grantchester, out through the Backs and along the Cam, with the trees growing down to the water and, beyond the river—really just a stream at this point—the flat, nearly featureless landscape of the fens. It was subtle almost to the point of tedium, beautiful in an extremely soft, understated way, rurally peaceful but within striking distance of a town, therefore civilized even in its state of nature. Just like England itself, she reflected. Sometimes they would cut across the fields on the paths which had been set aside as right-of-ways for casual strollers, kept sacrosanct during centuries of farming. Other times they would stick to the main road. Once she reached out to touch some "nettles," as he called them—they looked harmless enough—and was shocked at their enduring sting.

One evening, when they were still just getting to know each other, he'd brought her with him to the computer lab where he did the complex calculations for his dissertation. They'd been on their way out for a drink, and he'd asked if she minded making the twenty-minute stop. "It's the time when no one else is using the computer," he explained, "so I'll be able to get the results much more quickly."

She agreed readily, eager to see where he worked. And when he had unlocked the heavy outer door, and led her down several green-and-white corridors, and typed a long sequence of numbers onto a screen in the terminal room, and finally punched the button that sent them off into the machine's giant maw, he turned to her with an anticipatory look. "Let me show you one of its tricks," he smiled. "Name a date in history, any date."

"January 22nd, 1901," she offered.

He typed it in, pushed a button, and waited a moment. "A Tuesday," he read from the screen. "What was it that happened on that Tuesday?"

"What? You mean you don't know?" There was a strong element of teasing in her excessive surprise. "The death of

Queen Victoria. How can you not know that? She was *your* queen, after all."

"My queen? *My* queen?" With each repetition, he exaggerated the Cockney accent more. "I don't even consider Elizabeth 'my' queen. You know my politics. I think the whole bloody monarchy should be abolished." And he grinned at her, as if to cement their revolutionary conspiracy.

Paul lived in a College-owned house with two other graduate students he knew only casually. A couple months after she'd first become friends with him, he gave a party in his room, inviting everybody he'd met by then. She came, bringing Adam for comfort. Only when she saw Paul's quickly hidden expression of disappointment did she realize her mistake: he would think Adam was her boyfriend. So she hastened to rectify the error, explaining that she and Adam knew each other from college, that he was the only other American here she liked, and that he was just a friend, a *good* friend, but . . . She trailed off as Paul smiled, poured her a drink, and clinked glasses with her. "Cheers," he said.

Like everyone else at the party, she drank excessively and laughed and talked and stayed till all hours. People began to leave—Adam among them, waving to her from the door. At long last, when she saw that the party was beginning to empty out, she remarked to no one in particular that it was time to go and began to ease her way down the stairs. Paul, seeing her leave, followed her to say goodbye. Outside, on the few stone steps leading down from the porch, she tripped in the darkness (it was her inherited night-blindness) and nearly fell, but Paul caught her arm and held it the rest of the way down.

"Goodnight," she said at the bottom, turning to him.

"Goodnight," he said, kissing her cheek.

The next day she came to his room again, to help him with a Labour Party mailing. Through Paul she had become caught up in local politics. It excited her to think that a country could have, as one of its major parties, an organization that argued for democratic socialism. She had, at the age of eighteen, fallen in love with the ghost of George Orwell, and had sent a letter of condolence to his widow, who understandably never answered. (He had been dead about twenty years by then.) That beloved voice was what she now imagined she heard in the British Labour Party, and this was what Paul encouraged her to hear, grinning with complicity whenever a particularly articulate and appealing old comrade, preferably with a working-class accent, would sound the note he knew she loved.

Arriving to help with the mailing, she saw he had not yet cleared up from the party.

"Must do it tomorrow," he said, "or Edie will be after me."

The whole idea of College servants made her uncomfortable. In her own building, she had failed to face up to the issue to such an extent that she didn't even know her own bedmaker's name; she fled her room each morning before the woman came. Edie, who was toothless and ribald, made her particularly nervous. Paul, on the other hand, got along well with Edie in an easy, joking way, and never seemed to mind, despite his impeccable political beliefs, that he was benefiting from another's menial labor. It was *because* of his political beliefs, he explained

to her, that he didn't mind. Edie's work was work, just like anyone else's, and not to be sneered at nor shied from.

They sat among the empty bottles and overflowing ash-
trays and abandoned crumbs of cake, stuffing and sealing envelopes in their own miniature version of an assembly line. He
had cleared a space for them at his desk, the one place in the
room not covered with party debris, and they sat side by side,
he stuffing, she sealing, keeping up a flow of pleasant, calm
chatter to pass the time, until finally the once-enormous pile
of fliers had dwindled to nothing.

"Finished!" he said, pushing himself back from the table.
She too relaxed. Then he put his arm over the back of her chair
and, before she could even anticipate it with pleasure, leaned
over and kissed her.

They kissed for a few minutes from their respective chairs—
warmly, but uncomfortably—and then moved over to the bed.
Shedding their clothes, they burrowed under the covers. Paul
had a small, thin body and exceedingly soft skin; she had never
met another man whose skin was so smooth to the touch. Like
many of her college friends, she was always on birth control
pills—sometimes pointlessly for months and even years—just
to be ready for the occasional, unexpected moments when they
would prove necessary. So there was no hesitation, no delay, and
he was inside her in a moment. He commented on how wet she
was, so quickly, and she blushed.

When they woke in the morning, they were still surrounded by the empty bottles, this time with the sun shining through the colored glass and casting blurry lights against

the walls. They looked out from the bed and laughed at the vision of glorious disarray. At twenty-two and twenty-three, they felt themselves to be thrillingly decadent, that first Sunday morning in bed together.

"But," said Paul, "there's one thing I think we should agree on."

"What's that?"

"You know, after that bad relationship I had with Eva, I swore I'd never get involved with anyone else from my own college. And now I have—and I don't regret it." He gave her a quick kiss. "But it will be easier on us and less of a strain generally if we don't let other people in the college know we're involved."

"But why?" She didn't want to let him know that he was in danger of hurting her feelings. Even to herself, she couldn't fully acknowledge that she might feel hurt. All she knew was that for some reason his plan struck her as unreasonable, unfair.

"I just know it will work out better that way. Otherwise they'll begin to treat us differently. As a couple. You'll just have to take my word for the fact that things will be much easier if we do it this way. It doesn't make any difference to you, does it?"

"No," she said slowly, "I guess not."

"Good," he said, and kissed her again.

IT WENT ON that way for quite a few months. They would see their friends together, usually in a large group, and then the two of them would sneak back to her room (or, occasionally, to Paul's) and spend the night together—not every night, but two or three out of the week. If she was at Paul's, she would have to wake up early enough to get out of the house before any of his housemates saw her. This irked her, but not sufficiently for her to try to alter the arrangement: she believed, though not on the level of conscious thought, that if she insisted, she risked losing Paul. And she was still too young to take seriously the implications of being a hidden-away thing, a secret-life sexual embarrassment, for at that point in her life she had not yet had an affair with a married man.

And there were other problems, in any case, for her to focus on. The moment she began sleeping with Paul, their friendship deteriorated badly. Every remark of his became an occasion for taking umbrage, every quirk a bad habit she wished to change. Before, they had enjoyed their arguments about science versus literature, England versus America, male versus female, psychological versus practical reality. Now these things all became fraught. Everything was personal. And this, too, he objected to, because he felt it was she—with her American, psychological, literary femaleness—who was making everything personal.

She objected to his smoking. This was partly self-assertion (she had never been with a man who smoked, and she did not want to be with a man who smoked), and partly genuine concern, for the lung cancer reports had by then become all too clear. He might have said: You presume too much in thinking that we will still be together forty years from now, when I die of lung cancer. But he did not. Instead he simply asserted his right to continue indulging in his own bad habits. This she in principle acknowledged, but underneath she couldn't give it up. So one day, when he was elsewhere in the house, she took his half-empty packet of cigarettes and flushed it—flushed *them*, one by one—down the toilet.

When he returned to his room he looked around briefly and then said, "Have you seen my fags? I thought I left them here on the table."

She was nothing if not honest. "I flushed them down the toilet."

"You did what?"

"I didn't want you to smoke any more, so I flushed them down the toilet."

His face darkened in rage, but he said nothing more. He just turned away from her, with his lips pulled tight, and went about what he had been going to do.

She stood this for about three minutes, and then broke in, "Are you angry at me?"

"Of course I'm angry. Wouldn't you be?"

"Then why don't you shout and scream at me?"

He turned to her then with his Englishness full in his face. "Civilization," he rebuked her coldly, "consists of not shouting and screaming when one is angry."

Several times that year, he would nonetheless be brought to a shouting state of rage. It was not she who would bring him there, but Harold. Harold was one of Paul's two housemates. The other was a handsome but unreliable man named Ted, who didn't strike her as very interesting or even likable, though he was perfectly polite to her. But Harold was different.

Harold, with the canniness of the crazy, could get to Paul in a way she could not. In response to Harold, he would capitulate temporarily to the craziness, allowing himself to depart briefly from his strict rules of civilization. Still, Paul did not consider these departures significant. He didn't think anything connected with mad Harold could be significant. But she, when she thought back on this period, saw the incidents surrounding Harold as a sort of high-powered lens which magnified—at least to her own eye—the intense and irremediable differences between herself and Paul. And years later, thinking about it again, she saw something more. It was Harold who had eventually served as her model, Harold whom she was imitating, though unconsciously, as she sought to hold Paul's attention when the love affair waned. She had learned from Harold how to make Paul angry when she couldn't make him feel anything else.

But that was later. For now, in the early months, she was a mere bystander.

Whenever she was over at the house (which she was quite often, officially as Paul's good friend), she was very conscious of herself as the only woman among men. This was even true when Ted had a girlfriend over, since they—those vacuous blondes who paraded through Ted's bed and life—never really seemed to count, particularly with Ted. Ted had his string of blondes, and Paul, of course, had her (she was sure that Ted, at least, suspected this). But Harold had only his dog, a spindly-legged, yappy creature that was short-haired almost to the point of hairlessness.

He also had his work, as a research student in anthropology, and his job, as a bus conductor. "Being a bus conductor is a very specialized skill," Harold would say. "A lot of people just don't have the knack for it. Now, me—I'm a natural. The first few days it was sort of difficult—it is for everybody—but once I got everything coordinated, I was perfect. You know, you get to know the regulars—where they board, what their fare is, even which ones are smokers— and when they hand you a ten-pence for an eight-p fare, you have the tuppence all ready along with their ticket. It's all a matter of coordination. But I've seen blokes who couldn't get it right after six weeks. They were still fumbling for the change and having trouble with the ticket dispenser and holding everything up."

He delivered this speech to her one Sunday, not for the first time, as she sat in the kitchen of the house waiting for Paul to go out with her on their Grantchester walk. Harold was still wearing his uniform, minus the cap, as he stood over the grease-spattered stove stirring vegetables in a frying pan. On the other side of the kitchen, Ted and his current blonde sat at opposite sides of the grimy, paper-strewn table. The blonde, her mascaraed eyelashes still full of sleep grains, clutched a cup of black coffee. Ted slumped over the *Observer*, his hairy legs showing beneath his red terry-cloth bathrobe, his coffee cup empty on the table.

"Get me another cup, will you, love?" he mumbled without looking up.

"Get it yourself," snapped the blonde. "I'm not your bloody servant."

"Well, aren't we liberated this morning." Ted rose slowly, an air of self-righteous injury inherent in his posture, and poured himself another cup.

"Punctuality—that's what I try for." Harold's voice had taken on a higher, tighter note, verging on a quaver or a whine. "It's important to keep the bus going right on schedule. When we get to a stop, the bus stays for fifteen seconds—no more, no less. If the old lady on the upper level can't make it down in time, too bad for her. She can get off at the next stop. I try to hurry them along—give 'em a helping shove sometimes— but once in a while there are people who still don't make it."

Ted sputtered into his coffee.

Harold turned on him and yelled, "What's so damn funny? Who do you think you are, laughing at my job? I'd like to see *you* up at five a.m. every bloody morning. Not you—you're never out of bed before ten. And no use to anybody for an- other two hours after that." Then he turned on the blonde, as she giggled. "That goes for you too! Selfish bitch—can't even get someone else a cup of coffee."

"Oh, stuff it, Harold. What I do is none of your business. And if you think there's nothing to laugh at—"

"Shut up," said Ted. His girlfriend glared at him but stopped.

"Jesus!" Now Harold had turned on Ted. "What gives you the right to order her around? You treat people as if they only existed for your convenience. When you want to be nice, fine— you're the nicest bloke in the world, and everybody loves you. But once you've got people under your control, you really let them have it. Then the real Ted comes out—"

Paul appeared in the doorway and stood there for a second as if held back by the volume of tension filling the room. He caught her eye, and she responded with a glance that conveyed both her discomfort and her bystander status. Then he interrupted Harold. "Something's burning."

"Oh, fuck," said Harold, turning back to the stove and scraping violently at the pan of vegetables. He grabbed a plate out of the sink, emptied a potful of still-mushy rice onto it, and dumped the contents of the pan on top. Then he turned off the gas. He picked up the plate in one hand and a fork in the other and headed toward the door, calling, "Dolma! Come, Dolma!" The dog uncurled itself in the corner of the room and trotted after him. Harold pushed against Paul slightly as he went through the door.

"No need to shove," said Paul. Harold turned around quickly, and in doing so spilled some of his meal on his uniform jacket. He looked down anxiously. Then he looked up in response to Paul's unwilled snort of laughter, his scraggly hair framing his face as his mouth opened jerkily.

"Fuck you!" screamed Harold. "You're laughing too, now? You don't know a thing about real work. You and your socialist politics! I'm the only one in this house that has any real contact with the working class. The rest of you sit up here in your ivory tower and read books and program computers. Well, one day your computers are going to take over the world—and I hope they kill you first!"

He stood still a moment, his face about ten inches from Paul's. Then he ran out. The others remained silent, listening to the rattling of the iron spiral staircase as his feet pounded up it, canine toenails clicking along behind. Paul grinned and shrugged.

"Don't worry about it," said Ted. "Harold's always flying off the handle. He's half-Italian, didn't you know?"

A few days later she was sitting at the kitchen table, companionably reading, while Paul cooked his specialty dinner—bangers and beans—for the two of them. Ted passed through the kitchen and lingered a moment, almost as if he wished they'd invite him to join them. But Paul, it seemed, meant to remain resolutely silent. Or perhaps she was misinterpreting both Ted's pause and Paul's wordlessness.

"I haven't seen Harold around," she commented, settling for polite conversation. "Where's he gone?"

"Not that we're missing him unbearably," Paul chimed in.

"No, it makes a pleasant difference, doesn't it? He's gone down to London—to his parents', I think. Said something about taking Dolma home to his mother because she's sick."

"His mother?" Paul teased.

"No, Dolma, you idiot."

"You mean Dol-l-lma. Must pronounce it in the proper Indian manner, you know. Harold has a fit if you don't."

"Well, whatever-the-fuck-her-name-is is sick. I happen to know because she vomited all over my floor the other morning. The pleasures of having a room that adjoins Harold's. When it's not incense coming through the door, it's a sick dog. The damn bitch peed in my room last week, and Harold wouldn't even clean it up. 'It must have been your fault,' he says. 'You must have scared her or something. She never pees in my room.' That's a great answer, I must say. Of course she never pees in his room—she's emptied her bladder all over the rest of the house before she even gets up there."

"Christ!" said Paul. "If she ever did it in my room . . . I don't see why we have to put up with this. I mean, we could just go to the College and have the dog thrown out. It's illegal, and Harold knows it."

"Harold may bloody well know it, but he'd never forgive us if we did that. That dog is about the only living thing he cares for—west of India, that is—and if we got rid of it he'd never speak to us again."

Paul went back to cooking, and Ted left the room. She remained immersed in her novel, only vaguely conscious of the feelings their conversation had stirred in her. Then Paul broke in on her silence.

"I don't know how Ted can stand the bloke. When I first moved in here, I thought of myself as reasonably mild-mannered. I mean, I never hated anybody in my life. But I think maybe I hate Harold. He has got to be the most inconsiderate person I've ever met. I mean not just rude, but really thought-less. He couldn't care less about the rest of the world—Harold is the only one that matters to him."

"He is selfish," she admitted. "But not in the same way you or I would be. There's something impersonal about his self-ishness, something almost not human, or not normally human. And he's certainly not stupid. I've heard that Edmonds personally recommended him for his research place, and though Edmonds may look like an old drunk, he's probably the most respected anthropologist in Britain. Being a research student of his is nothing to sneer at. And it was Edmonds who got Harold that travel grant to pay for his trip to India."

"Oh, his Indian pretensions!" Paul's impatience was clear. "That's one of the things that really gets me. The way he wears that Indian bedspread wrapped around him, and eats that foul vegetable-and-rice dish for every fucking meal. You know what he did the other day? I was walking out to the shed to get my bicycle, and all of a sudden I hear a shout—probably supposed to be 'Watch out below' in Hindi or something—and then there's this whooshing noise and a loud 'splat,' and I look down and right next to me, not five feet away, there's a pile of soggy tea leaves. He just throws them out the window. I mean, Christ, where does he think he is, back in the village or something? He is such a slob! I've never seen anybody live in filth like that. You know, Edie won't even clean his room any more. Not that he'd let her, even if she wanted to. Last night I went up there looking for our big pot. It was the first time I'd been inside his room for ages. There's a kind of funny stench, part incense, part dirty laundry. And that bed—just a mattress on the floor covered by a dirty blanket. And the bathroom was unbelievable. That's where I found the pot, caked with three-day-old rice, and a trail of ants going in and out of it. Gorgeous. I just left the pot up there. Dead loss, it was."

His rant had been so long, and so uncharacteristic, that it left a strange after-silence in the air when he was through. She broke it by asking, half-humorously, "Are you quite finished?"

And Paul, who was never very far from ironic self-mockery, grinned sheepishly. "I suppose that will do for now."

———

"Today's seminar is about ritual as a key to society's moral attitudes." Harold cleared his throat and continued. "I propose to examine the general topic by looking first at a specific example: marriage ritual in the isolated highlands of India."

Ted smirked at Paul across the dining room table, then hurriedly assumed an air of reserved interest as Harold looked over at him. She and Paul exchanged glances. Harold frowned.

"But first we'll eat. I think the meal should be just about ready now." He got up from his place at the head of the table and went into the kitchen, where he made several loud clattering and scraping noises.

"Do you need help, Harold?" she called.

"No!"

"Just offering," she said under her breath.

"I can't believe I'm sitting here," muttered Paul. "But at worst it will be a good laugh."

Ted winked in agreement, then spoke up in a loud, stagy voice. "These lunch seminars are a great idea. Since we're all doing different subjects, we can really teach each other a lot."

"Here it is," Harold announced, coming back into the room with a small pot in one hand and a medium-sized frying pan in the other. He set the frying pan directly on the wooden table and spooned approximately two mouthfuls of rice from the pot onto each person's plate.

"Gigantic portions," Ted noted.

"Well, I would have made more, but I couldn't find the big pot." Paul choked. "Anyway, this is the best part." Harold ladled out the fried mixture, which was a uniform greenish-brown color, and sat down himself. They began eating.

"Mm, delicious," she said, feeling that someone was obliged to do so. "What do you call this, Harold?"

"Food," answered Harold. "Just food. That's the direct translation. There's no specific term for it because this is all we eat out there. Very nutritious. I lived on nothing else for a year and a half." He gobbled up his plateful in about forty-five seconds and looked up at the others.

"Slow eaters, aren't you?"

"Well, Harold, why don't you start reading while we're still eating?" Ted suggested, poking tentatively at the pile with his fork.

"All right, if you're sure you'll be able to concentrate."

"Oh, of course," said Ted.

Harold cleared his throat again and began to read, enunciating every word with particular care. The first few paragraphs were entirely theoretical, with long quotations from Lévi-Strauss and frequent uses of specialized vocabulary, and she found her mind beginning to wander. What am I doing here, anyway? she thought. I don't live in this house. But then her attention reverted to Harold, who—now on about his third page—had started describing the marriage rituals in India.

"In this rural society, women are a scarce commodity. When a young girl marries a man, she is essentially marrying the whole family. All the brothers, and the father too, have conjugal rights. They are all her husbands, and therefore they all have an interest in forming the marriage." She sensed herself growing uncomfortable, and then felt embarrassed at the presumptuousness that underlay the discomfort. "The entire family raises the sum necessary to pay the bride price," he continued. "In the particular village under study, this price ranged from two goats to thirty thousand rupees. The highest price was demanded by the father of the most attractive and intelligent girl in the village. However, by the time I left the village no worthy husband had been found, and as each year passed the girl would lose some of her value with increasing age."

Harold looked up and changed to his normal speaking voice. "Actually, I almost married that girl. Her brother and I were close friends. In fact, we'd been through the blood-brother ceremony and had sworn perpetual loyalty to each other." She couldn't help thinking, as he said this, that Harold's version of India sounded a lot like a little boy's fairy-tale kingdom. A fleeting suspicion that he had made up all his fieldwork passed through her mind, and then she mentally castigated herself for the unjustness of the suspicion. For all she knew, life in rural Indian villages *did* resemble a fairy tale. "He wanted me to marry her, and so did her father, and they would have lowered the bride-price to fit my finances. She was really a wonderful girl, too. I was very tempted, but it would have meant staying there forever, and at that point I wasn't ready to commit myself. Sometimes I wonder if I didn't make a terrible mistake."

The telephone rang in the other room and Ted, who was sitting nearest the door, got up to answer it. Harold resumed his reading, but almost immediately Ted came back and said, "Harold, it's for you."

He jumped up and, as he passed her chair, bumped rudely yet obliviously against her, as if she were a piece of furniture. When he'd left the room, she turned to the other two and said, "I like the way he apologizes to me so profusely. Just because I'm not the most valuable girl in India . . ."

"Oh, he likes you well enough," Ted assured her.

"Likes me! He barely acknowledges my existence."

"You should consider yourself lucky then," said Paul.

"You know what I think?" she said, realizing what she thought even as she put it into words. "He's jealous. He hates me for taking away his friends, as he sees it—for taking up even a smidgen of your time."

"Oh, come off it," said Paul. "We don't owe him anything."

"Well, he seems to think you do."

"What do you think *mamma mia* is calling about?" Ted remarked, in a not-very-subtle effort to change the subject.

"Oh, undoubtedly a health bulletin on the stupid dog," said Paul, obviously grateful.

The telephone receiver banged down loudly, and Harold ran through the room. His face was streaming with tears. He rattled up the spiral staircase, and they heard a thump on the mattress and convulsive sobbing.

"It's dead," she said.

"Good riddance," said Paul.

———

A few weeks after the dog died, she was sitting alone in Paul's room preparing for her next day's supervision on *Troilus and Criseyde*. She liked Chaucer—a surprise, since she had avoided him all through college—but was never quite sure how to take him. Where was the firm morality she had learned to expect from nineteenth-century novelists? Were Chaucer's people good or bad? Did they deserve their fates, or not? He would never say.

She'd barely seen Harold since the day of the tragic phone call, and had heard nothing specific about him (Harold not being one of Paul's favorite voluntary subjects of conversation). She had the feeling, though, that he was getting even weirder, progressing from merely eccentric and difficult to downright morbid and withdrawn. From what she could gather, he hardly even came out of his room these days. The good side of this, if there was one, was that Harold and his housemates hadn't had a chance to clash over anything new. Nor had there been any recent opportunities for him to treat her with his habitual oblivious rudeness.

Suddenly there was a soft knock on the door, more a scuffle than a knock, really. She called, "Come in?"—the rising tone indicating that she had never really believed someone was there. But the door did open, upon Harold.

He looked strange, stranger than usual, all shaggy and wild-eyed, with his Indian bedspread half off, and she was a little scared. She was sitting in Paul's only comfortable chair, the overstuffed armchair by the electric fire, and she just contin-

ued sitting there and looked up at him from her book and
didn't say anything. Harold didn't say anything at first either.
He came over and stood right in front of her. Then he dropped
down on his knees, put his hands in a clasped gesture of prayer,
bowed his head over them, and said, "Forgive me."

She managed to mumble out something to the effect that
it was all right—whatever *it* was—and then he jumped up and
ran out. The whole incident left her feeling disconcerted, and
a bit scared still, but also very sad.

It was a few days later that they all received Christmas cards
from Harold. (It was late January by this time.) The cards bore
a picture of a bus on the front, and had "Merry Christmas" and
the previous year's date inscribed inside, along with Harold's
full signature. The signature was hardly necessary, as Paul
pointed out, what with the bus and all.

The Sunday after that, she was once again waiting in
the kitchen for Paul to take their walk, despite the cold and
gloom of the day. Paul came down wearing his long overcoat and the green mohair scarf she had, in a fit of atypical
domestic virtuosity, crocheted for him at Christmas. She put
on her coat as well, and they were just about to go out—had
already turned, in fact, to say goodbye to Ted, who was sitting as usual over his coffee and Sunday papers—when
Harold came downstairs. It was the first time they'd seen him
downstairs in weeks.

"This place is a filthy mess," he announced. (It was true that
things could have been a trifle neater. Edie didn't come on week-
ends, and by Sunday the common living areas always had an
overly lived-in air. But this was nothing new.) "Nobody around

here cares how it looks except me," he continued. "Nobody else does any work to clean it up. If we're all living in a house together, we ought to cooperate to keep it clean."

He looked at the three of them and they looked at him. There was total silence for about five seconds.

"You filthy bastard!" Paul burst out. "Who are *you* to talk about keeping things clean? You! The dirtiest person in this house! With that stinking room, and those cruddy rice-caked pots, and those grimy feet that—"

"Be quiet, be quiet," said Harold, nervously wringing his hands together.

"I *won't* be quiet. It's time someone told you off. For you to talk about cooperation, about thinking of other people, is the most hypocritical thing I've ever heard. If you had one ounce of consideration—"

"Be quiet, I tell you! Stop it! Stop it!" Harold turned and grabbed a glass from the kitchen counter, then raised it over his head and brought it down on the counter with a violent crash, as if it were a gavel. Glass shattered to the floor, and the room went dead quiet. Harold stood looking at his bleeding fist. Then he grabbed the door handle with his other hand, pulled the door open, and ran out. Blood spots on the floor marked where he had cut his feet on the broken glass.

"You'd better go see if you can help bandage him up," she told Ted, when they had all had a few seconds to overcome their shock.

"Why me?" he asked.

"Because he probably won't let anyone else near him. Oh, for God's sake," she answered his put-upon look, "I'll go, but don't be surprised if he throws me out."

"We'll both go," said Ted.

They started up the stairs, Ted in the lead. Paul stood by the door, dressed for outdoors, his mouth still open as if in mid-sentence. When he began speaking, they both stopped on the stairs and turned back toward him. "I didn't think he'd— I didn't know—"

"Don't worry about it. It's just a tantrum," said Ted. "In Italy they do this sort of thing all the time."

For days they heard constant typing overhead. Then pieces of paper appeared throughout the house. In the dining room she found a challenge to Paul—"would oblige me by meeting for a duel on the fifteenth of this month at two of the afternoon, weapons and location to be chosen by yourself. As for seconds . . ." On the kitchen table they found a fairy tale, a long and rambling account of Prince Harold and the beautiful goldenhaired Princess Astra, both imprisoned in an old castle filled with demons and surrounded by a moat containing vipers. And all over the house were fragments of Harold's thesis, incoherently elaborating strange theories on the significance of ritual. Harold, having made a vow of silence on the day he cut his hand, kept it when convenient, breaking it only to ask for impossible-to-obtain items on the rare occasions when he emerged from his room for food.

And then one day Paul returned home from the computer lab to find her crouched on a chair by the kitchen table, her knees pulled up to her chest and her shins jammed against the table, her arms clasped around her legs and her head hidden in her arms.

"What the hell——? What's the matter?" He shook her rather roughly by the shoulder.

She looked up. She was beyond tears; frozen.

"They came to get him."

"They? What do you mean? You mean Harold? Where's Ted?"

"He went to London this morning. Then there was a telephone call from Edmonds. He said he's been getting weird, affectionate letters from Harold, announcing that Harold has disproved all his theories, and he wanted to know if anything was wrong. I told him about the typing and a little while later he came over with two men from Fulbourne. When they went up to see Harold he yelled at them for calling him Mr. Black and told them he was Dr. Black, and he showed them a certificate he'd typed out awarding himself a PhD. Then his parents came and they all took him away to Fulbourne and he was screaming that they had no right and he wet his pants and I didn't know what to do. . . ." She lapsed into silence and hid her head in her arms again.

"Christ!" said Paul. "Jesus Christ!" He stood there absently patting her on the shoulder. Her paralyzed state obviously repelled him. He clearly saw it as some kind of alliance with Harold's unreasonable behavior, a further extension of the household's recent tendency toward neurosis and melodrama, away from the quiet sanity he valued and insisted upon. None-theless, sensing his responsibilities, he stooped down and put his arms around her.

"Look, there's nothing you could have done. Come on, don't be upset. He's probably a lot better off there. He obvi-ously couldn't take care of himself at this point."

She relaxed a little in his arms and he rocked her slightly. "That's right. Don't worry. It'll be fine. It'll be a lot easier for us here now that he's gone. No more rows. No more mess. And none of it was our fault—he was just crazy. Now, are you feeling any better?" He kissed her. "That's right. Nothing to worry about. After all, we're still here, right?" He kissed her again, and then began to unbutton her blouse. And though she didn't at all feel like it, she let him.

When she thought about that winter, in the years to come, she remembered it as a cold, dark time. Other people might have recalled it as the winter of the miners' strike, when of-fices were lit by candles and even Piccadilly Circus went dark for a time. But for her it was the winter of Harold's madness.

THAT SUMMER SHE was back in America. She had a job offer that she thought might lead to a career. (Erroneously, as it turned out: she was eventually to choose a different career.) And she needed the money, since she couldn't work in England. Also, she had had a series of dreams—public humiliation dreams, of the appearing-on-the-street-naked variety—that suggested to her she needed to go back home for a while, to let up on the strain of constantly behaving with the very slight degree of unnaturalness required of her in England.

It was the summer of Watergate, or rather the second summer of Watergate, at the end of which (though she couldn't have foreseen this) Nixon was to resign. She took almost no interest in these public events. She rode the subway to work each day, fed the cats at her various house-sitting jobs, and read. She started with *Anna Karenina*. When she finished that, she began *The Golden Notebook*, which irritated her enormously. Perhaps it was merely the comparison with Tolstoy, a competition any modern writer would lose. But she felt the source of her irritation lay deeper than that.

"I prefer D. H. Lawrence," she announced to her friends, at any rate those who would listen. "At least he has some sense of what's at stake between men and women. If the men are all as bad as Doris Lessing thinks they are, then what's the point?"

At other times she would say, "This sexual politics stuff reduces everything to the lowest common denominator, as if all our individual personal problems could be solved by legislation, or the proper social conscience. But that isn't the kind of problem *I* have with men. It's not so much that they're too powerful; more often they're too weak. And anyway, each case is different, and the power problems don't sort out so easily into men versus women. It's a matter of one person against another. And it's *necessarily* that—that's what Lawrence understood."

So she became a bore on the subject of feminism and literature.

"Lighten up, " one male friend said to her. "*The Golden Notebook* is a wonderful book. You can take it to parties and meet a lot of great women."

And her women friends just said, "You don't understand. You don't understand what it is to be a victim."

Paul wrote to her. Not often enough, but he did write. She would seize each letter, tear open the flimsy airmail envelope, and scan the pages quickly for anything personal. There was rarely anything she counted as that—nothing that would qualify these as love letters. But then he had never said he loved her. Still, she would skip quickly to the end to see if he had written "Love" before his signature. No. He never had. Then she would go back to the beginning and read the letter slowly, for content. He always spoke of his work, his evenings at the pub with mutual friends. Once he mentioned having gone to the movies with a male friend and two secretaries from the chemistry department. She quivered with anxiety, then told herself she was being foolish. If he mentioned the date in the letter, how important could it be?

She went to the Upper East Side one Saturday and got her hair cut. This was at the instigation of one of her college friends, Anne, a dependable sort who was now in law school.

"He's very good," Anne said of her haircutter. "It's a little expensive, but the salon is very nice, and he's really very good. A little faggy, though."

"I won't notice that. I've been in England all year." They both laughed.

It *was* a good haircut, but it only made her feel that the rest of her was unkempt. Too much effort and money, she thought, would be required to keep all the different parts up to par at once. Better to give up on the whole thing now, and not bother.

Adam passed through town on his way from Washington to Boston, where he was visiting friends she didn't know.

"Nice haircut," he commented.

She told him the joke about the haircutter and England, since he too had been there and would understand. He laughed drily, briefly—a stiff little laugh drowned out by her own loud chuckle. She reminded herself that she had never been very good at telling jokes.

They went to dinner at a place in the Village, escaping from the muggy night to an air-conditioned semi-cellar. She complained to him about Paul. He commiserated, but reservedly.

"He doesn't feel things very strongly," she said. "Do you think it's because he's a scientist?"

"I doubt it." Adam smiled. "Maybe you feel things too strongly."

"Do you think so?"

"I don't know. What are we measuring against? There's no correct standard. It's just a matter of finding the right match."

"And you think he's not the right match for me," she accused.

"How can I judge? I hardly know the man. I'm just going on what you tell me."

"It's true I only tell you the bad parts. But that's natural. There's never really anything to say about the good parts. It would sound boring or sappy."

Adam smiled then, that characteristic smile in which one side of his long, wide mouth looped up higher than the other. His smile, everyone said, was the most endearing thing about him. It gave his otherwise severely handsome face a slightly goofy quality.

He looked down and fidgeted with a bit of parsley left on his plate. The gesture gave her time to admire the length of his eyelashes, the strong streak of his eyebrows against his high forehead. Then his glance met hers, and he was serious again.

"The one thing I've never been able to get is why he insists on keeping it all a secret. I mean, everybody must know. Surely his roommates know. And I know other people think—"

"You haven't told anybody about this, have you?"

"Of course not. You know I wouldn't, when you asked me not to. It's just that people know I'm a friend of yours, so they mention it to me. The other Americans, especially, think it's very odd that you two take such pains not to look like a couple, when it's obvious you are. They think—"

"Oh, the other Americans! I don't care what they think?"

"You imagine you've become British?"

From anyone else she would have taken it badly. From Adam, though, she could see it as a wry joke.

"Yes, one of those obnoxious ones with the fake accent." They both laughed, and then she grew sober. "It's not that he allows me to become British. It's more the opposite—that when I'm with him, my Americanness seems special, unique, rather than something I happen to share with a lot of boorish tourists and aggressive warmongers."

"Hardly a comprehensive description of our compatriots."

"No, but you know what I mean. It's easy to fall into that way of thinking over there. And when I'm with Paul, I feel as if I've been singled out for the good side of my Americanness—my energy, my raucous sense of humor, my straightforwardness—you know. Things that seem run-of-the-mill here."

Adam nodded. "But the secrecy?" he pushed. "Doesn't that ever bother you?"

Now it was her turn to gaze down at her plate. "No, not really. It's just something he wants because of the way things worked out with his last girlfriend. And it doesn't really matter much to me." When she glanced up, she saw that he was scrutinizing her closely. "I mean, I guess I'd *prefer* it if we could be publicly affectionate and all. But it's not really a major gripe."

When he left after dinner, he gave her a kiss on the cheek. "See you in the fall," he said.

She watched him as he walked away, as he turned and waved before going down into the subway entrance. Funny, she thought. Adam is much more attractive than Paul, and much nicer. Why am I in love with one and not the other? She knew it was a stupid question.

Paul arrived late in the summer to pay a three-week visit. She had been looking forward so much to this that inevitably it was a disappointment, at least at first. He looked so small—not just when she met him at the airport, but later that same day when they went to a dinner party she'd been invited to. *Hold your own!* she kept wishing at him silently, while the fluent and intense academic conversation poured over him. But he was like a rock in the midst of a river (or a pebble, if she was to insist on his smallness), allowing the conversational waters to flow on either side of him but finally not altering their course. She, on the other hand, took up every topic, had a response to everything. *Why can't I be with a man more like me?* she asked herself, and felt her hosts asking about her. But then she provided her own answer: Because in that case he wouldn't be able to stand me. Nor, she hesitantly admitted, I him.

The next day his reticence came out again, as they stood in line—or rather, in the undifferentiated crowd—waiting to order their lunch at a local deli. Being English, he insisted on ordering for her; but being English, he couldn't push himself up to the counter with the necessary vigor, couldn't outshout or outshove the demanding Americans who clamored around him. For twenty minutes they waited unserved. Then she took matters into her own hands and shouted out their order. He ate the meal she'd won for them, but boiled silently all the while.

That night they had their first fight of the visit. It was also the longest and most painful fight they'd ever had (painful, at least, for her—she couldn't speak for him). She started it by asking about the date with the secretary from the chemistry department.

"Did you sleep with her?"

"Well, yes," he admitted. He did not say it as an admission, though, more as a statement of unsurprising fact.

"How *could* you?" she screamed. "I *knew* it. I knew it the second I read the letter."

"Well, but why shouldn't I? We didn't say we wouldn't sleep with other people."

"What does that have to do with it? How could you even think I would sleep with someone else?"

"Why not? We're not married."

"That has nothing to do with it." But it had everything to do with it. She felt married to him, even if he didn't to her. Felt it the more *because* he didn't, and his explicitness made the situation all the more painful.

"Didn't you think about my feelings at all?" Tears were streaming down her cheeks by this time. "Didn't you even wonder how I would feel when I read that in the letter? Oh!" She clutched her heart. "It hurts so much, I can't tell you." This was not melodrama, but banal truth; or rather, it was melodrama only insofar as melodrama can also be sincerely felt.

He paused to think, as he always did, and then replied thoughtfully, in what she considered his most scientific manner, "I'm sorry if I hurt you. That was never part of my intention. But I don't think I can run my life by what will hurt you and what won't. For one thing, I can't predict with any certainty how you'll feel—"

"Did you honestly not think this would hurt me? How could you possibly think that? Don't you know me at all?"

Again he paused. "Whether it would hurt you or not, I was going to say, was not a question I felt bound to ask myself. I didn't feel it was any of your business what I did while you were away, or while we were away from each other."

She invoked lawyer's logic. "Then why did you tell me about it in a letter? Why did you even mention the secretary, if it didn't have anything to do with me?"

"I suppose I felt that it's always best to tell the truth. But that makes it seem far more conscious than it was. I was just reporting on my activities to you, that's all. That's how I write letters. I don't try to calculate, with every sentence, what effect it's going to have on the person reading it."

"And that's what's wrong with you. You *should* do that kind of calculation, or at least more of it than you do. A letter isn't a message in a bottle, you know, thrown out for some stranger to find in the distant future. It's a personal expression from one individual to another. Usually an expression of *feeling*, though you wouldn't know anything about that."

This time his pause lengthened into a silence. She stormed out of their borrowed living room (a feeble imitation of marital domesticity, this house-sitting) and into the bathroom, where she threw cold water on her face. Then she stormed back in again. "Why don't you answer me?"

"I thought your comments had reached the point of pure attack, where they didn't require an answer."

She gave an inarticulate snarl, of anger or pain—it was hard even for her to tell how much of each went into the feeling that possessed her.

They went to bed furious, hunched at the very edges on their respective sides of the queen-size mattress. In the morning they were tentative with each other, polite. By afternoon, though, the fight seemed to have worn off, and they made unexpected, restorative love on the living room carpet. For one short moment during their lovemaking she pictured him doing this with the secretary. That's the trouble with sex, she thought. All bodies do it approximately the same way. But the thought didn't lead her anywhere useful, so she hurriedly covered it over.

That evening, as they watched on the TV news, Nixon announced his resignation. It was, by this time, not a surprise. Others had predicted it—others who had been glued to the hearings all year, who had made household names of the Watergate operatives and the governmental interrogators and the assorted players in this nationally televised drama. She, in her year in England, felt she had broken away from the nation and its dramas: a colonist repatriated in the mother country, a rebel against the rebel. But she could savor the pleasure of the Nixon resignation as well as any American. Her first vote had been a fruitless one for McGovern, cast against the landslide of 1972. She was happy to see the misery in that dewlapped, beetle-browed face as it announced its impending departure from the White House.

And afterwards they watched an old British war movie, one that Paul had seen before and loved. Actually, it was an anti-war movie, with heroes dwindling and dying in the face of their own side's cruelty and corruption. But like all anti-war movies it shared a great deal with its opposite: the bleak setting, the uncomfortable quarters, the moments of high tension punctuating long periods of inactivity, the focus on a small group of individually defined, variously appealing, uniformly male characters.

Paul kept saying, "Isn't it good?"

The film's self-evident goodness seemed to make him happy, animated, whereas it only made her increasingly miserable. She wanted to fall asleep, to escape from these men and

their horrible, inescapable situation. But the movie wouldn't
let her. She was gripped. She had to see how it all came out,
though she knew it would come out badly. When it did—
when the most heroic and complicated figure had been put to
death by his superiors—she burst into tears.

Paul was impressed but bewildered. Having praised the
film throughout, he could not now say, "It's just a movie!" But
she could see he wanted to. He waited for her tears to stop.
When they did not, his bewilderment turned to irritation. He
closed his eyes and breathed in imitation of deep sleep. She
continued to sob quietly, self-pityingly. She wanted him to put
his arms around her, comfort her, say it would be all right. But
if she had to ask, there would be no point. She wanted him to
understand, without her saying it, that these national tragedies,
these deaths of soldiers and misdeeds of presidents, were not
objective, historical events. Any access they had to the tragic—
any tears they could cause to be shed—were due to their personal nature, to their effect on individuals. Their effect, if it
came to that, on her.

And then, back in England, it was the fall of the Cambridge
rapist. Such a funny country, she thought, only one rapist in a
large university town, so he gets to be THE Cambridge rapist.

For months women were advised not to walk alone in the
city after dark, not to stray on country paths even in broad
daylight. It irked her. One of the good things about England
had been the freedom to come and go as she pleased, fear-
less, independent. Now even this aspect of America was

seeping in, poisoning her new life, reminding her of old restraints.

For months they sent around fliers of a terrifying-looking creature with a heavy black beard. One of her Scottish friends— muscular, bearded—had repeatedly been stopped by the Cambridge police and forced to submit to blood tests. But in the end the perpetrator turned out to be a rather frail-looking fifty-two-year-old family man (the beard was a disguise) whose wife hadn't a clue. How could you not know about someone so close to you? she thought, and then thought: Only in England.

When they caught him, there was nearly a riot. She watched from the window of her sitting room in Peas Hill Hostel as they sneaked him out a side door of the Town Hall, his head covered by a cloth bag. Meanwhile, around at the front entrance, hundreds of women stood chanting and held signs: "Death to Rapists!" "The Solution is Castration!" "Take Back the Streets!"

It was also the fall of the national elections. The day after she and Paul got back from America, they'd been drawn into the frenzy of the Cambridge Labour Party. It seemed odd to her, the attitude they took toward their local candidate. Everyone acknowledged he was a drip (a "berk," they usually said). Yet somehow he had been selected. And, they assured her, it didn't matter that he was a drip. Once elected, he would pretty much have to vote the party line; he was bound by the platform. All this worry about his personality was, they felt, a bit American. It wasn't the man that mattered, it was the party. And if you wanted Labour to win this time, you had to vote locally for Jim Driscoll. He was, indirectly, your only means of voting for a Labour prime minister; there was no other vote available to you. Not that any of them liked the prospective Labour prime minister much better. (And how did *he* get to be leader of the opposition, she wondered, if everyone disliked him so much?) But even the prime minister's personality didn't matter that much, they said, because he too was bound by the platform. It was that simple.

She signed up to canvas the local citizenry. Not one in twenty asked about her American accent. Possibly they thought she was from another part of the country; the British could be weirdly provincial in that respect. Or maybe they just assumed she was an American who had married an Englishman and adopted his citizenship, like Winston Churchill's mother. At any rate, they listened—politely, for the most part—to her Labour Party spiel, and sometimes agreed to tell her how they were planning to vote. She marked down these responses on the list of addresses she carried with her. This was the real point of canvassing, she'd been told. On election day her lists would be used to get out the Labour vote—by personally driving people to the polls, if necessary.

Some of her political work she did with Paul, including envelope stuffing. It lacked, however, the romance of their first night together. Now it was just work. Everything about their life together (though "together" hardly described the simulation of separateness he still insisted on)—everything, these days, lacked romance. Daily he grew colder, harder, more withdrawn. She responded by becoming whiny and demanding, more emotional, more pathetic. As she could have predicted, this made him even colder.

The night after the election (Labour had won), they sat facing each other in her ugly little sitting room. It was only October, so she hadn't bothered to turn on the two bars of the heater. They still had their coats on, having just come in from a late dinner at the cheap Greek place. The overhead light glared down on them, inspiring the flowered upholstery with an almost manic oppressiveness. She waited for him to speak, but he did not.

It wasn't that they had just had a fight, or at any rate not a designatable, specific spat. It was all more futile and desperate than that. Feeling was seeping away from them. It was as if someone had made an irreversible mistake, as if something had gone terribly wrong, but so slowly that you couldn't pin down the moment when they had ceased to be in love with each other. Not, she reminded herself, that he had ever told her he loved her. Nor, for that matter, that she had ever stopped loving him, or would ever stop. But hers was now a desperate, demanding, unreimbursed sort of love that only made her unhappy.

She imagined she could feel his desperation as well, even from across the room. He wanted to leave her but was afraid to say so. He hated tears, and he knew she would cry if he did this. He was weighing his options, rationally trying to decide which course of action would result in the least pain and embarrassment—pain for her, embarrassment for him. And pain for him, because for him embarrassment *was* pain. Yet he felt trapped and unable to choose. She sensed all this coming across the room from him and she decided to save him, by acting herself.

"Do you want to break up?"

He started guiltily. "Do you? What makes you say that?"

"I can feel it in every gesture of your body, every expression that crosses your face. You don't want us to be together any more. You feel trapped." At this he looked aside, but she went on. "I can't stand it when you're so cold to me. It would be better to be apart. I could stand that better."

He was quiet for a moment. For longer than a moment, it seemed to her. He always took so long to formulate his thoughts into sentences. At this particular juncture, it seemed an added cruelty.

"I don't know what I want. Can you understand that? I'm confused, and I can't sort out my feelings."

"So you want me to do the sorting for you? Is that it? One of us has to do something. We can't just go on like this, both miserable."

"I wouldn't say miserable, exactly—"

"Well, I would. You're not good at knowing what you feel, but I can see it. I can tell you want to break up. Don't you? *Don't* you?"

He simply shrugged, and looked at her with sad, watery eyes, and looked away again.

"Well, if you want to stay together, then say so. You must want one or the other. Do you want to be together?"

This time he didn't even shrug. He just continued to look away, into the cold bars of the electric fire.

"All right, that's your answer, then. I have to say it for you. That's it. We're splitting up." She was not crying. She could at least do that.

He was, though—barely, but visibly, his tears filling the corners of his eyes as he looked at her. "Are you sure that's what you want?"

"It's what *you* want. But I'm the only one with the courage to say so. All you can do is sit there and be miserable."

At this he stood up. "This is it, then. If I go now, we're through, once and for all."

"Oh, yes, pretend it's *my* fault. You know it's what you want." Now her voice rose to a shriek. "Get out! Get *out*, I said! You got what you wanted. It's over. Now get out!"

He walked out the door and closed it softly behind him. As if that had been her cue, she burst into tears. The hour grew later, and the room grew colder, but she continued to sit there and weep as if she were never going to stop.

In the morning she felt ill. Her throat was sore, her head throbbed, and she felt dizzy when she tried to stand up. She spent the day in bed. When the bedmaker arrived to clean, she harshly told her to go away.

But the next day the bedmaker returned with the senior tutor of the college, and he in turn brought the college nurse. They took her temperature. The nurse felt behind her ears.

"You've got glandular fever," she said, "and we've got to move you to the college infirmary. Come along, I'll help you get dressed."

She felt, though, that if she left her room Paul would never be able to find her. Whatever she did, she had to stay exactly where she was. It was not certain he would come back, but she had to be there in case he did. If he were to come back and find her gone, he would feel let off the hook. He would not bother to look for her. Or (the fever made this difficult to puzzle out) he might want to see her again, but he wouldn't know how to. He would never find out she had gone to the infirmary. She would die there—of glandular fever, whatever that was—and he would never know.

"No!" she cried. "No, I can't! I can't leave here. I have to stay. I can stay here, can't I?" She turned to the senior tutor, who had once loaned her twenty pounds from the college emergency fund when her check from home had failed to arrive on time. He had seemed kind at the time. "I can stay here, can't I?"

Confusion and compassion mingled in his face. "Er—nurse?" He looked to the uniformed woman for help.

"No, you cannot," she responded crisply. "We must keep you where we can watch over you, and give you special meals. And where it's warm. You'll like that, won't you? It's just across the road here."

"But how will anyone know where I've gone? No one will know. No one will be able to find me there."

"Nonsense, dear. We'll tell your friends. They'll all come visit you. Would you like us to call one of the other Americans?"

"No! No, we can't call. No, please leave me here. Please."

Now it was the nurse's turn to look questioningly at the senior tutor. He brightened with his solution.

"Look here, we'll leave a note on the door. Right? Now I'll just go into the next room to write it—paper and pens in the desk drawer, I assume?—and Nurse Watkins here will help you to dress. I'll do it right now."

She was too tired to protest. Weeping, she got out of bed and let the nurse dress her. The tutor returned with the note and taped it to the door, averting his face so as not to seem to notice her tears. Together they bundled her into a coat, helped her across King's Parade, and led her to a tiny room that she had never known existed, somewhere behind the pantry. The last thing she remembered before falling into a heavy sleep was the quaint antiquity of the iron bedstead.

Adam was there when she woke up. Some flowers sat on the bedside table in a green glass vase, with a card propped against it.

"From you?" She looked from the flowers to his face.

"No." He handed her the card. "From your comrades." Inside the card it said: *Best wishes for a speedy recovery from the Cambridge Labour Party.*

"This is from me." He handed her a package wrapped in a Heffer's bag. Peering in, she saw it was *The Wings of the Dove.*

"My favorite! And how funny. I—"

She paused so long he had to prompt her. "You what?"

"Nothing." She shook her head. "Nothing. Just a dream I had, I guess, but I can't really remember it. You know, like a feeling of déja-vu." She opened the book at random to a page in the middle. "I haven't read this for years . . ." But when she tried to follow the long, thick paragraph of print that now lay before her eyes, she couldn't make sense of any of the sentences. Then she remembered her illness.

"Oh, God! I have some kind of brain fever or something. What was it? Jugular—no, glandular fever. I can't even read. Do you think I might be dying?"

"Don't be ridiculous. Glandular fever is just the British name for mononucleosis. Didn't you have mononucleosis senior year?"

"Yes." She breathed it with a sudden relief.

"Well, you've just had a relapse. Anyway, what kind of friend do you think I am? Do you really think I'd bring a book about an American girl dying in Europe to an American girl dying in Europe?"

She laughed, or tried to, but it came out as a cough. At this the nurse bustled in. "I think that's long enough for today. We don't want to tire out the patient."

Adam rose obediently, and she was too exhausted to object. Instead she just gave him a faint wave of her hand, which he answered with a smile.

"Thank you," she said.

"Not at all. I'll be back."

"Good."

When he'd left and the nurse was tucking the sheets into the side of the funny old iron bedstead, she asked, "How long have I been here?"

The nurse looked at her watch. "About thirty-six hours. Are you hungry? We have a nice piece of fried plaice, and some veg, and a little pudding."

"I'm starving." And she was. But when they brought the fish she could only eat a few bites of it, and even that she threw up.

"Too soon for solid food," said the nurse. "But don't you worry. We'll soon have you up and well."

Paul did not come until her last day in the infirmary. He entered the room with a hangdog expression—but whether it was intended to cover his failure to appear earlier in her sickroom, their parting fight, or some other crime of which she was as yet unaware, she couldn't be sure. All she knew was that, even as he appeared, he was in hiding.

"So, you get out today." He was attempting to sound chipper.

"Yes."

She resolved to give him no further help, so there was a long pause. Sitting in a chair next to the bed, he looked down and began twisting the ends of his scarf—that green mohair scarf she had crocheted for him the previous Christmas. It moved her to see that he was still wearing it, but the emotion had something in it of anger.

"Labour seems—"

"Are we—"

They stopped simultaneously. She had been about to launch into something personal; he, as usual, was clinging to the broadly political. She decided to have her way.

"Are we still broken up?"

He looked hurt that she would even bring it up. Then he turned his head to the side and spoke as if to a third, invisible party in the room. "You know what I said."

"What?"

He sighed, as if exasperated at the childish persistence. "I said that if I walked out that door, we were through. I don't go back on my word."

"Oh, bullshit. This honor business is just an excuse to do what you want. Are you seeing someone else already?"

"Don't be ridiculous." He got up then, and pulled his overcoat around him.

"Leaving so soon?" she said nastily.

"My visit obviously wasn't bringing you any pleasure. I'll see you in the college dining hall, I suppose. But please don't make a scene in public."

"A scene? A *scene?*" she shrieked at his departing form.

The first thing she realized when she got back to her room after the four days away was that she had no money. She would need cash, if only to pay for her dinner that night in the dining hall. So she bundled up again and went back down the stairs and out to King's Parade, to the National Westminster branch half a block up the road. Inside, the bank was hot and stuffy. One of the tellers was smoking. As she approached the window, she realized that she was about to faint.

"Excuse me—uh—I have to sit down."

She pushed her way outside and, seeing no other place to rest, sat down on the curb. Mixed with her fear of fainting and the upwelling of nausea that was included in it, she discovered a streak of livid embarrassment. People don't do this in England, she thought. What will they think of me, sitting on the curb? They'll think I'm a drunk, or a maniac, or, worse, a crude American.

A man had followed her out of the bank. Now he sat down on the curb next to her. "Feeling ill?" he said.

"Yes." She smiled gratefully at his quiet voice, his civilized accent. "I just got out of hospital and I guess it was too early to be—"

"Quite. You feel faint, do you?"

She nodded.

"Best put your head between your knees, then. That's right. Just lean over. That will bring the blood to your head and keep you from fainting. No, don't sit up yet. It's all right—I'll watch to see that nobody runs you over."

She sat up smiling. "It's very nice of you to—"

"Not at all. A damsel in distress, and so forth. Can I ring somebody for you?"

"No." She scrambled to her feet. "No, I'll be fine. I live just up here. Thank you." She turned to walk away, and then turned back to wave at him. "Thank you so much."

"My pleasure." And did he tip his hat, or was that only a false memory she imposed later? When she tried to think back about the incident, she could never accurately recall his face.

When she was feeling almost better, she took a trip by herself to London. It was, she told herself, an exercise in self-sufficiency, an attempt to claim for her own a city which had been jointly possessed by the two of them. Let Paul have Cambridge; she would take the metropolis.

She got a mid-morning train and was pleased to find it was one of the old-style ones, with separate compartments of facing seats covered in green-plaid plush. The compartments were joined by a carriage-long corridor on one side, and on the other side each had a little door that led directly outside, so that you could exit and enter without going through the train. Like a Hitchcock movie, she always thought. Or your own little room on wheels. Meanwhile, another part of her brain desultorily considered the eternal train-ride question: Exactly what pastoral landscapes, real or imaginary, were being portrayed in those anonymous, wood-framed, nearly identical prints tacked up above the seats and below the luggage racks in each compartment?

Some prior occupant had left an old, out-of-date copy of the *New York Review of Books* on one of the seats. She picked it up hungrily and turned first to the letters page, attracted by the name of Susan Sontag. ("Against Interpretation" and "Notes on Camp" had been the scriptures of her freshman crowd.) Apparently Sontag, in an earlier issue, had reviewed a book by or about Leni Riefenstahl, and had used the occasion to launch into a major attack on the cinematographer's moral aesthetic. Now Sontag, in turn, was being attacked by some irate feminist for failing to respect the work of a fellow female. She was pleased by Sontag's reply: something to the effect that feminism ought not be a bludgeon with which to flatten all discriminations—that it was important to point out evil, whatever kind of body it inhabited. So there was still a discussion going on out there. One didn't *have* to begin and end the conversation about women's rights with who did the Hoovering or the washing-up. She felt a twinge of homesickness for that America, with all its silly, passionate attachments to ideology and self-examination. We may seem naive in our explicitness, she thought, but there are certain kinds of understanding that can't be reached implicitly. And there's an emotional bravery, too, in being willing to appear naive.

The flurry and bustle of King's Cross jarred her out of her thoughtful mood. It was necessary to decide, first of all, which tube station to head for. Adam had advised her to visit the Chelsea Physick Garden. "With a k," he said. "The beds are wonderful—they're laid out according to who discovered the plants. And if you go on the right day, you can even get tea." South Kensington, she saw from her map, would be the best bet, and she could get there on the Piccadilly Line without changing.

But it was a long walk through subterranean tunnels at the King's Cross end, and then another half-mile through the well-heeled streets of Chelsea after she had climbed the steps leading up from the South Kensington station. And it turned out, after all, not to be the right day. The public was allowed in only on Wednesdays and Sundays, according to the sign posted on the high stone wall that surrounded the garden on all sides. The wall was so enormous and forbidding (it took up an entire block, on one side of the street) that it intensified her desire to see the now-secret garden. Thwarted, and aware that she was in any case in a weakened state, she felt on the verge of tears. This is ridiculous, she thought. You don't even *like* flowers.

But then her luck changed. Two men in black suits and bowler hats walked past her on the sidewalk, acknowledging her with the superior, apologetic smile common to their caste and country. One of them pressed a buzzer by the locked door, and a man in a different sort of suit answered. Then each of the two bowler-hatted gentlemen (they appeared not to be together) explained his reason for seeking entrance, and each was motioned in. She followed them, announcing, "I've come all the way from America, only to find . . ." Without waiting for the end of her excuse, the doorman waved her in. By the time she emerged from the vestibule, the two men had mysteriously disappeared; she had the garden to herself. Most of the leaves had already fallen from the trees, the plants were mainly scrubby and grey, and there were no flowers in bloom. But as she walked up and down the paths, reading the idiosyncratic labels on each bed, she felt herself growing calm and rested. Her solitude was a desirable state here, not a penance.

Something of the same feeling, but this time much more intense, came over her toward the end of the day as she walked across the Hungerford Bridge. It was twilight, London's best hour, and the dying light was gleaming on the river, which stretched far into the distance toward the faintly visible Tower

Bridge. On the bank behind her, as she turned her head, she could see the rooftops of the City, with St. Paul's rising in their midst, while in front of her lay the concrete-and-glass façade of the Royal Festival Hall, England's charmingly ineffectual attempt to sound the note of architectural modernity. London was all before her. She was tempted to linger on the bridge to prolong her immense feeling of well-being, but she needed to get to the Hayward Gallery before it closed at six. It was already five-fifteen when she paid her admission fee, and she hurried into the galleries to catch the small but fine European Romanticism show.

It was in the room where Henry Fuseli's *Nightmare* hung that she had what later struck her as the distinguishing experience of the day, the event that in retrospect cast its tone over the whole expedition. She had been sunk in contemplation of the painting—not only because of its own gripping qualities, which showed up so much more clearly in person than in any reproduction, but also because of its tenuous links with the life and work of a writer she much admired. Then she became aware that another woman—older than she, very English-looking, with a bony but attractive face and straight brown hair—was also staring at the Fuseli. She turned to look at the other woman, who gave her that polite British smile. That should have been the end of things, by rights. One didn't address strangers, not in that place, at that time. But something, perhaps a lingering remnant of that expansiveness from the bridge, got into her.

"Would you like to know an interesting fact about that painting?" she asked.

At her words, the woman turned to look at her again, full in the face this time. She looked younger and less brittle than in profile. They were the only two people in the room. "Please," said the woman, in her polite way.

"The man who painted that painting lived with Mary Shelley's mother—I mean, years before Mary Shelley was born, he was her lover. And even though Mary Wollstonecraft died in childbirth, so that Mary Shelley never knew her own mother, you can see in that painting a kind of ghostly ancestor of *Frankenstein*. See?" She pointed at the canvas, indicating the white female figure draped across the bed, the monster perched on her chest.

The other woman turned back to the painting and stared hard. "Yes," she said, "I see. I shall always remember that. Thank you."

It was this response—the quaint, unironic phrasing of it, and also the intense if abbreviated communion it implied— that she recalled all the way home on the train to Cambridge, and for days and years to come. It was so English. It reminded her of everything she had ever cared for in this strange, ridiculous, admirable country.

Paul was civil with her, even friendly. He smiled pleasantly enough when he saw her at meals, laughed at her occasional witticisms, offered to do small favors (none of which she accepted, though she allowed others to do much more). As she recovered her strength and vivacity, they almost seemed to move back into their old friendly relation, as it had appeared in public. And privately he at any rate did her no harm. There was never even a whisper of his seeing another woman. But he did not come back to her room, ever. He did not allow the private side of their friendship to resume.

She was among those he invited to his shared house for the annual Guy Fawkes celebration. Ted and Paul (and, the previous year, a rather manic Harold) had got into the habit of holding a bonfire in their own backyard, and then a party. Last year she had stayed over after the party as a matter of course. This year she could assume no such privilege.

Dressed warmly for the crisp November night, she made her way out to the house by bus. It had been dark for several hours when she arrived, but the party was just getting organized and she was the first guest on the scene. Ted, his latest blonde in tow, clapped her on the back affectionately and then, unable to resist overdoing it, kissed her on the cheek. The blonde simpered hypocritically. The third roommate, Harold's female replacement, was absent—away at the biochemistry lab as usual, Paul said. She could detect from his tone that this woman, at least, was no threat.

"Oh, thanks." Paul took the bottle of Spanish red she'd brought. "We can use that."

"When do you light the fire?"

He looked at his watch. "Give it another half hour, I'd say. A number of people should be here by then. Enough to enjoy it, anyway."

The fire, when it did go up, produced an appreciative gasp from the twenty or so friends who had assembled by then. She stood next to the Scotsman who had been repeatedly mistaken for the Cambridge rapist. When she shivered he put an arm around her, mistaking her apprehension for cold. Later he got her a cup of mulled wine, and seemed willing to stay by her side as long as she needed him. But he abruptly moved away when Paul approached—like a wolf cowering before the head of the pack, she cruelly thought, and then laughed at the idea of Paul as a bloodthirsty patriarch.

"What's so funny?"

His half-smile and his crinkled eyes, softened by the flickering of the fire, made him look positively friendly.

"Nothing," she answered. "I was just thinking about what kinds of animals we'd all be, if we weren't human."

"Ted is a snake, I suppose."

Now she laughed again, in acknowledgment. "And his new girlfriend is a fluffy little chick, ready to be eaten."

"Andrew must be a big, furry dog of some kind," Paul said, referring to their bearded Scottish friend.

She glanced at him in quick admiration. "You're good at this. What kind of animal am I?"

"Not so fast. You first, it's your game. What am I?"

She looked at him and thought for a moment. No, it definitely wasn't a wolf. It was something quiet but forceful, small but tenacious, soft but with claws. "Maybe an ocelot."

"An ocelot! Why?"

"I don't know. It just seemed right. Not a domestic cat, but something along those lines, only untamed."

"I like the idea of untamed."

"Not in the sense of wild or uncontrollable. But not susceptible to the usual human entrapments."

At this he looked warier, but still interested. "Dangerous ground here. But let me return the compliment. You are a . . ." He narrowed his eyes. "A fox."

"How odd that you should say so."

"Why? You don't see yourself as svelte, quick, crafty, and easily frightened?"

She laughed. "And capable of terrorizing henhouses. No, what makes it odd is that my best friend when I was five years old—the little boy who lived down the street—called me Foxy because I reminded *him* of a fox."

"Ah, well, obviously a young man of discernment."

He had to go then to attend to his other guests, but he pressed her arm warmly as he moved away. This she took as a sign of encouragement. She stayed on as the other guests started leaving. Late in the evening she found Paul again in the kitchen, indulging in yet another glass of wine. She accepted a glass from him and they sat down to argue the merits of a movie each had seen separately the week before. As usual, they disagreed.

When at last the friendly argument had run its course, they found themselves alone in a silent house. Everyone else had gone or gone upstairs.

"Well," said Paul, "quite a successful party, I'd say."

"Very."

He looked at his watch then. "Christ! It's gone half past one. You've missed the last bus back to the city center."

"Have I?"

But he wouldn't respond to her flirtatious tone. He was angry now, suddenly and deeply angry. "Bloody woman! You've done this on purpose, haven't you? Thought I'd let you drift back into my bed and start up the whole thing again. But I won't do it. I won't be manipulated that way. You'll have to stay, I suppose, but you'll stay on the sofa downstairs."

She was shocked into silent acquiescence and merely sat in the kitchen while he frantically collected blankets, sheets, and a pillow. Then he led her into the sitting room, which looked out through a large glass double door onto the dying embers of the bonfire. "There," he said, and slammed the door behind him as he went upstairs.

She took off only her outermost sweater and covered herself with the blankets. But she was too shaken to sleep. She imagined herself as some Little Red Riding Hood figure, taking shelter under the roof of a dangerous predator. That wolf again.

After about twenty minutes she heard footsteps on the stairs and the door to her room creaked open. Good, she thought. He couldn't stick with it. He's come to apologize, or maybe even to make up.

But one glance at his face, in the cold, white moonlight that came through the glass doors, told her she had been wrong to hope. He was still angry. His anger had solidified and grown confident of itself, taking over his entire body so that as he began to shout at her he was quivering with rage.

"What is it that you're trying to do to me? Can you tell me that? Why do you tie me in knots like this? I can't seem to explain to you," and here he enunciated each word slowly and carefully, as if speaking to an idiot or rehearsing lines in a play, "how very much you upset me. I cannot tolerate it. I do not want to feel like this. You make me—you make me want to hurt something! My God, you make me want to hurt *myself.*"

At this he turned from her toward the wall and slammed his fist into it with all his might. The wall shook but didn't crack or dent. His hand, she could see, was bleeding.

"You see that? *That's* what you make me want to do." And he turned, white-faced, and rushed out of the room.

She had never seen him strike anything or anyone before, had barely ever heard him raise his voice. This was not the Paul she knew but some stranger who was capable of violence. She threw off the covers, put on her sweater, found her coat in the hallway and, drunk as she was and cold as she increasingly felt, walked the two miles back to Peas Hill.

The next time she saw Paul was two days later at lunch. When she had gone through the cafeteria line and paid for her grey beef, her overcooked veg, and her pudding drowned in runny custard, she emerged into the vast space of the dining hall and looked around for a familiar face. She spotted two. Unfortunately they were located at the same table as Paul. Well, she thought, I'm not going to be beaten that easily. No reason why *he* should walk away with all our friends.

The other two greeted her warmly and asked about her health. Paul was silent. He concentrated on his food and continued to say nothing until the other couple stood up to go. "Coming for coffee in the bar?" one of them asked.

"In a minute," Paul said. "First we need to have a word in private."

She had already stood up herself, but sat down again now—hesitantly, questioningly, and dazed by his sudden eruption into intimate public confession. Or so it seemed to her. But the others took it as normal and waved a temporary goodbye.

"What?" she said when they'd left.

"I think we have to get a few things straight so this doesn't happen again."

"So what doesn't happen?"

"Us ending up at the same meal table with each other."

"And why shouldn't we? I have a right to be here too, you know. It's my college just as much as it is yours." She could feel herself growing shrewish, but that didn't stop her. "They're my friends too. Just because it's your goddamn country doesn't mean—"

"Keep your bloody voice down."

His angry face, as much as his remark, shut her up.

"All right," he said. "That's the point. That's why we have to work out a procedure. Now, I suggest that whoever comes in second is responsible for sitting at a different table."

"Great. So you get in here first and grab all our friends every time. Two can play at that game. I'll just arrange to get here early every day—"

"Fine. Whatever you want. If you like we can even divide up the lunch period between us, and I'll always come in the second hour."

"No, that's not fair, because most of our friends eat later. So you would always get more of them."

He was silent with rage. After about ten seconds he said in an artificially calm voice, "I am attempting to be rational about this, but you obviously don't want to cooperate. Have it your way. But until things calm down between us, I don't want to have to sit at the same table as you. Is that clear? If you do sit down at my table, I'll simply be obliged to get up."

"Fine with me. And how about the coffee bar? Or the Cellar Bar in the evenings? Are you going to leave the second I come downstairs for a drink?"

"I don't think that's necessary, as long as we can ignore each other."

"I can ignore *you* well enough. But what I can't ignore is if you bring other women in here. I'm just warning you, this is my house and if you bring other women into it that will be a real violation."

He got up from the table and turned away. His back, as he walked toward the door, emanated controlled fury.

She knew she was being unreasonable, but she believed she had a right to her unreasonableness. Her rage was epic, irrational, unbounded. She felt an urgent need to vent it. As Paul turned to go into the coffee bar, she jumped up from the table and went out the other door to the cloakroom. There she searched the racks until she found it: the green mohair scarf. Stuffing it under her own coat, she ran out of the building, through the main gate, across King's Parade, and up the steps to Peas Hill. Breathless, she unlocked the door to her bedroom and hid the scarf among her sweaters in the bottom drawer of her bureau.

Was it a week later, or a month, that she committed the public atrocity? In retrospect she could never get the timing straight.

It was certainly sometime before Christmas. But whether it was in late November or December she couldn't afterwards recall—perhaps because, in the early days after the incident, she had done her best to blot it out entirely.

It was, at any rate, a Saturday night. She had finished her work for the following Monday's supervision and found herself at loose ends. Even her books repelled her. *Great Expectations*, which she was reading for the first time, filled her with an unwarranted depression over Miss Havisham's fate—surely an idiosyncratic reaction, she realized, springing only from her own exaggerated sense of having been recently abandoned at the altar. And *Sons and Lovers*, which she was re-reading, inspired her with alternate pangs of sympathy and annoyance. Mired in one of Miriam's endlessly repeated (though, she felt, quite justified) complaints about her lover's neglect, she at length threw down the book and set off for the Cellar Bar. There would certainly be people she knew there on a Saturday night, and the glass or two of cider would make it easier for her to sleep.

She didn't like bars in America, and though she didn't mind British pubs, she would never think of going into one alone. But the Cellar Bar was different. Located just downstairs from the dining hall, it had the homey feel of being part of the college premises. During the daytime the room was used for other functions—she herself had briefly taught a dance class there, her first year—so it had the virtue of familiarity. And at night it was lit so that it felt welcoming whether it was empty or full, early or late.

This time she hit the evening in midstride. The room was sprinkled with people drinking and talking. It was an oddly diverse collection, from the college hearties (sporting their purple and white scarves) to the scruffy leftwingers, and including along the way the studious scholarship boys, the leggy freshman girls, and the affectedly Edwardian late-blooming aesthetes, most of whom did their best to resemble Oscar Wilde. It always amused her to see this gathering, and it pleased her now to see several of her friends—two Australians and Andrew, the bearded Scot—drinking in their midst. They raised their half-empty glasses to her as she approached with her full one.

"Cheers," she answered, feeling slightly foolish as she always did when adopting the local pub jargon, but aware that it would have been rude not to. They bantered about the quality of the beer and the length of the aesthetes' hair and the boredom of Saturday nights in a provincial university town. It was all very superficial, but it calmed her nerves and made her feel rested.

Just then he came into the room. She couldn't help feeling an irrational lift of her spirits at seeing his face, despite the fact that she knew they would have to ignore each other. Behind Paul was Ted, and between them, hidden at first by the two men's bodies, was a slight, dark, serious-looking woman. Not Ted's type, she couldn't help realizing. Pretty but not flashy, and without a trace of the requisite subservience.

"Who's the girl?" she whispered to Andrew. "Is that the new biochemistry roommate?"

"Don't know," he answered. "Let me find out."

He turned to his other side to consult one of the Australians, and then turned back. "Says it's one of the secretaries in the chemistry department. Kind of cute, isn't she? Not Ted's usual type, though."

She could feel her face change color, but whether she was blushing or blanching she couldn't tell. She saw Paul turn to the dark girl and evidently ask her what she wanted, leaving Ted to get his own drink. Paul made his way to the bar, eventually obtained two pints of bitter, and returned to the small, serious woman. Clutching her own glass of cider and riveted to the floor at Andrew's side, she watched all this with the intensity of an eagle focusing on its next meal.

"Big drinker for such a little thing, isn't she?" said Andrew. Then he set down his empty glass. "Excuse me a moment. Just need to pop out to the toilet. Can I get you another drink on my way back?"

"No, thanks."

Andrew's departure acted on her like a physical release. She was no longer bound to that spot on the floor. Still holding her glass, but too dazed even to think of drinking from it, she drifted slowly across the room toward Paul and the secretary. The woman's back was to her, and even Paul didn't spot her until she was practically upon them. His face hardened, but he composed it quickly into civility. He said nothing, however.

"I thought we had a deal."

"What do you mean?" The frown had returned to the space between his eyebrows.

"You promised you wouldn't bring other women to the Cellar Bar." She didn't even glance at the secretary as she spoke, though she could feel the woman's eyes on her. This chit was nothing. It was all between her and Paul.

"I promised no such thing."

"You did, the last time we spoke. Remember, I warned you. I told you it would be a violation—"

"Go to hell." He had already turned his eyes away from her, back to the dark-haired woman. He was getting ready to ignore her. Without thinking, she chucked the contents of her cider glass into his face.

He gasped, with surprise at first, and then with speechless rage. The people standing closest to them sensed that some drama was occurring and stopped chattering, but the wider buzz of the room still prevailed. Before Paul could say or do anything (but what would he say or do, in this situation completely beyond his experience?), she turned away and walked quickly toward the door. She felt as if everyone was looking at her but could see that in fact many were oblivious. Her heart was beating very quickly—almost, it seemed to her, loudly. Her face felt flushed. The feeling inside her, welling up as if to burst her, or burst out of her, had the warmth of embarrassment. But it was not embarrassment. That would come later. What possessed her now was the temporary, delusional thrill of victory.

It was cold when she woke up. Still cold, as it had been the night before when she put on flannel pajamas, a heavy sweater, wool socks, and even a knitted cap for extra warmth. Unexpectedly cold, though it was like this every morning. In her sleep, she had been back in the heated bedrooms of America.

She squeezed open her eyes and looked gummily at the clock. Ten-forty. If she hurried, she could still make it to the library by eleven, in time for cheese scones and morning coffee. It was the little things like cheese scones that made survival possible.

"Would you think I was being melodramatic if I said that the little things like these cheese scones are what keep me going these days?" she asked Adam as they sat on a bench in the corner of the library's inner courtyard, grasping at the few moments of weak morning sun.

"Yes," he said. "I would. But what's wrong with being melodramatic?" He took another bite. "And they *are* good scones."

"They're the only thing that gets me out of bed in the morning. Otherwise I'd just lie there in a state of depression all day."

"You know, you don't actually seem that depressed to me. Except, of course, that you're always saying you are."

"Well, when I'm talking to you I'm always less depressed. That's usually when I'm eating cheese scones. But you should see me when I'm alone. God, am I depressed then."

"If a tree falls alone in a forest, is it really depressed?" He gave her a quick grin, and she punched him lightly in the side. He flinched—even, it seemed, before she touched him.

"You know what this makes me think of, sitting out here in the courtyard?" He gestured, with a nod of his head, at the grim brownstone walls that enclosed them on all sides. "It reminds me of the time I stayed overnight in prison during the 1970 March on Washington."

"Oh, yeah, I remember that march. Spring of freshman year. But no one I knew ended up in prison. How'd you manage that?"

"It was a whole group of us, including one of our professors. We just refused to disperse fast enough, so the police rounded us all up and took us to jail. It was only for that one night."

"Was it scary?"

"Actually, what it was was incredibly irritating. You'd be trying to get to sleep around two in the morning and some group of maniacs would begin chanting, 'Ho Ho Ho Chi Minh, the NLF are going to win,' or whatever."

"Adam the great radical," she laughed.

"I never claimed to be a great radical. I was just against the war."

"I know. Me too. And now they're finally getting out. I feel so cut off from it all, over here."

They were both silent a minute.

"Are you looking forward to being back home again next year?" he said.

"No. I mean, I don't know. I'm miserable here, but I don't want to leave. I've applied to do a PhD here, and if I get a fellowship I'll probably stay."

"Why, if you're so miserable?"

"I don't know. Something in me loves this place—I mean, loves England—in a way that's deeper than rational explanation. When I first got here last year I felt in some strange way as if I were coming home, even though my ancestors, God knows, had nothing to do with England."

"Maybe it was all the old English novels you read as a child," he suggested. "I read them too."

"Maybe. Maybe that was it."

It seemed years before it was no longer winter. Then, unbelievably, it was spring—so much so as to be almost summer. She had never seen green like the grass of the college lawns or the new leaves on the trees shading the Backs. It was no doubt an English specialty, the kind of thing that made Shakespeare characters chirp on about "this emerald isle." Was it a trick of the light, or an actual variation in the photosynthetic element? Perhaps it was simply that the eye, starved for color after the long, grey winter, heightened its own response. She couldn't be sure. But it did seem to be a greener green than anything she'd ever seen in America.

It was late in the afternoon on the day of the King's May Ball. Cambridge, with characteristic disregard for the common calendar, always scheduled its May Balls in June; and King's, as if to announce its further dissociation, refused to hold a formal ball. Instead there would be an informal party, a series of discos and film screenings and buffet suppers and beer-and-wine bars, occupying the various public rooms of the college. She had promised to go with Andrew.

It was not that she didn't like Andrew. She liked him quite a bit, actually. But he didn't seem made for romance. No, that wasn't fair. There were hundreds of women who would be capable of falling in love with him. Thousands, maybe. Objectively speaking (if one could speak in such a way about attraction,

which one couldn't, but nonetheless), he was far better looking than Paul. He just wasn't made for romance with *her*.

It wasn't for lack of trying, either. They had been out on the
requisite dates. They had even tried going to bed a few times.
She, at any rate, had tried; Andrew appeared to have succeeded.
It wasn't that she found the experience unpleasant, exactly. More
that it failed to touch her in any way. Unlike merely physical
sex, it wasn't even a source of relaxation, for her anxious worry-
ing over why she couldn't fall in love with Andrew always
prevented her from coming. He, however, didn't seem to notice. And that too was part of the problem. Since she liked him,
she hadn't yet wanted to hurt his feelings by calling it to his
attention. But her failure to tell him compounded his failure
to notice, pushing them farther apart than ever. If things continued along in this manner, even her liking for him might
soon disappear. Tonight, she figured, would have to be the
showdown.

As the afternoon light faded into early evening, she poured
herself two quick shots of port. Something about the rich,
sweet taste of the drink seemed to match the golden light of a
Cambridge sunset, and as her winter depression had eased, she
had allowed herself to fall into this habit. A port or two and
some chocolate-covered digestive biscuits at six-thirty or seven,
then dinner or, as in this case, an evening out.

She did not think she was an alcoholic. There had never
been any alcoholism in her family, and she did not appear to
be a prime candidate for that particular addiction. She was,
after all, capable of waiting: until the depression cleared, until
the sun began setting. So it was not a necessary crutch, the

way the cheese scones and Adam's conversation had been all through the winter. But it was a definite pleasure. She did not, like most of her American acquaintances, smoke grass. She had never dropped acid or even sniffed cocaine. So she felt she deserved this one minor vice. Drinking made her feel relaxed. It also, she was convinced, made her more amusing to be with.

She dressed for the evening in something that fell into the sizable middle ground between a party dress and a costume. It was a sheer, black, clingy gown with an uneven hem of see-through ruffles and a bodice of appliquéd flowers. With this, she wore heavy eye makeup and a little lipstick: another aspect of costuming. Her long, heavy hair fell loose around her shoulders. Glancing in the mirror, she decided she hadn't looked so alive for months. She must finally have gotten Paul out of her system.

Andrew arrived at about eight-thirty, looking endearingly, bearishly dressed up. In his large paw he carried a small flower—a corsage for her, he announced. She excused herself from wearing it on the grounds that it would clash with the flowers on her dress, then put it in a cup of water to preserve his feelings. She offered him a port, which he refused, but she took the opportunity to have another small one herself.

She tossed it back in one flamboyant gesture, then set the sticky glass on her desk. "All right, ready to go."

"Aren't you going to rinse out the glass first? The dregs will never come off, if you let them dry on. Here, let me," Andrew urged, and was out the door before she could stop him.

"Good as new," he smiled as he came back from the kitchen, holding up the twinkling shot-glass as if it were a trophy. She smiled in return, but reservedly. She was going to have to say something soon to cool him down a bit.

"Andrew."

"I know, we don't want to be late. Let's go now. Do you need a wrap?"

"No, I'll be fine. Thanks." It could wait.

Several hours and four pints of cider later, she was standing at the edge of the Junior Common Room, which had been converted for the evening into a disco. She had, with some effort, managed to shake Andrew loose in order to gain a brief, solitary respite. He was probably still back in the film room, where she had left him with the announcement that she could not sit through *Some Like It Hot* one more time, much as she admired it.

In the course of the evening, she had run across most of the people she knew at Cambridge, or at least at King's. Adam had declined to come, though she had invited him, as she always did to events at her college. Paul she had seen here and there, looking furtive and secretary-less. Perhaps that episode was over by now. He and she had exchanged civil nods in passing, but no conversation.

And now she had the pleasure of anonymity. She stood in the shadows by one of the windows facing out toward the chapel, alternating her gaze between the still, serene view outside and the loud, clomping crowd within. The beat (early Rolling Stones) was so strong she seemed to feel the room vibrating to it. She sipped the last of her cider, feeling mildly, pleasantly sick. The music, the darkness, and the drink wrapped her up, secure and warm, as if in a cloak of invisibility.

"Dance?"

It was Ted, of all people, looking simultaneously dissolute and charming, in his usual untrustworthy way.

"Where's, uh—?"

"Cheryl? She's had it already, took the car back home. I told her I'd be up a bit later, not to wait up for me."

He gestured again toward the dance floor, one eyebrow cocked in invitation. She nodded, set down her drink, and joined him there.

To her surprise, he was a very good dancer. She didn't know why she should be surprised. Because he was English? Some of them had to be able to move. After all, they had a Royal Ballet Company. Because he was despicable? No logical connection there. Many of the best male dancers she'd known had a streak of caddishness; it often went with the territory. Why was that? She had just settled down to a lazy consideration of this question, which did not interfere with her ability to keep the beat, when the song suddenly ended and a slow dance began.

Ted stepped forward and put his arms around her. She was too surprised to back off—and, having acquiesced instinctively to the first step, she was pretty much committed to the whole dance, unless she chose to make a fuss. She settled her hands lightly on Ted's shoulders. He pulled her closer.

"I've wanted to do this for a long time," he whispered into her ear. She despised him, but the whisper tickled deliciously.

"Right," she answered.

"No, I'm serious. I've fancied you since the first day Paul brought you over. I could tell I wasn't your type, though—morally speaking, that is. Disdain was practically written across your face every time you saw me."

"Not—"

"Don't lie. It's not your style. That's part of what makes you so attractive." He moved his hands farther down her back, settling them in the curve just above her buttocks. "Only part, though."

"You know, Ted, you are a real sleaze." She was whispering almost as close to his ear as he had been to hers. "Your girlfriend goes home early and you take off after the first available woman—"

"Hardly. I've been waiting for this opportunity for months. Years. Anyway, you'd be capable of the same thing."

"Me?"

"Little Miss Innocent? Yes, you. I'm never wrong about people. I can always see inside them, even when they can't see inside themselves. And I can tell there's a devil in you. You're just aching to be cruel and irresponsible."

"The way you were to Harold?"

At this he let go of her and stepped back. He put his hands on her shoulders as if to hold her to the spot, and bent his head so his eyes looked directly into hers.

"You don't know the full story there, my dear. And you shouldn't judge what you don't understand. Harold and I have known each other since we were five years old, and there's a lot more between us than you could ever fathom. What you saw was the tip of the iceberg."

"Oh, right—and if I knew the rest I'd think you were Prince Galahad. So what's the story?"

"It's confidential."

"How convenient."

"I'd tell you if I could. It's not my secret to tell. Or not only mine. Anyway, it's all in the past."

"Oh, yeah? Well, how about the present? Harold conveniently disappears, and life goes on as before. I bet you don't even know where he is now."

"30 Elgin Crescent, basement flat. It's a halfway house run on pseudo-Laingian principles. I doubt that all the psychological mumbo-jumbo is doing the poor sod any good, but at least it gives him a place to live. And he seems to have settled in reasonably well."

"You've been there?"

"Every Sunday that I don't have to work."

She returned his direct glance. It occurred to her to say she didn't believe him, but she didn't have the nerve. And she wasn't sure what she believed.

"Better dance or sit down," he said. "We're making a public spectacle of ourselves." He put his arms around her again and this time she leaned into him.

"Not done in England," she laughed.

"Absolutely not."

At the end of the dance he whispered, "Let's go back to your room."

She was too chastened, by this time, to counter with her habitual self-righteousness. She hesitated.

"You know you want to. I can feel it. You've been bored

to tears, being dragged around all evening by that hairy git. It's been driving me mad—"

She snorted with laughter. "He's not a hairy git!"

"Then why are you laughing? See? You want to be as ruthless as I am; you just don't have the nerve. Tonight's the night. It will all be over tomorrow, and then you can forget about it. But for now, live a little."

"All right," she said, marveling at herself even as she agreed. "But I have to tell Andrew I'm leaving."

"Meet me by the Porter's Lodge." He blew a kiss and left the room.

She found Andrew, as she had expected, sitting plunked in front of the movie. Marilyn Monroe was in the process of steaming up Tony Curtis's glasses.

"Andrew, I'm really sorry but I have to leave. I'm starting to feel a little sick."

"Oh, no, is it a relapse?" Andrew's face expressed real concern. His kindness made her feel guilt, which immediately converted itself into resentment. The jerk, she thought, he makes lying too easy.

"No, nothing serious. I've just had too much to drink."

"Well, let me get my coat and I'll walk you home."

"Don't be silly. It's just across King's Parade. And I don't want to drag you away from the movie. Besides, I can be there before you can even find your coat, and I really need to lie down right away." She knew her selfish reason would be the one that persuaded him.

"Well, okay." He gave her a little kiss on the cheek. "If you're sure. I'll come by to see you tomorrow."

"Fine. Bye."

She felt like a real shit. So this is what Ted felt like all the time. It was kind of thrilling.

He was waiting for her by the Porter's Lodge, as promised. "Get away all right?" he grinned conspiratorially. Then he put his arms around her and she reached up and they kissed, a long, intense kiss, right there in the lit-up alcove by the college's main gate.

They had been in bed for less than an hour and she was well on the way to her third orgasm when there was a muffled tapping at her bedroom door. "Visitor for you," mumbled a sleepy voice that she recognized as belonging to the rather asocial geographer whose room adjoined the hostel's front door.

She wrapped herself in the quilt, leaving Ted with only a sheet, and opened her door a crack. It was indeed the geographer, pajama-clad and bleary-eyed.

"Bloke insists on seeing you now," he said. "I told him it was after midnight and he should come back tomorrow, but he wouldn't go away. Thought I'd better check with you before letting him in."

"Thank you. That was very thoughtful. I'll go deal with him now. Sorry to disturb you."

He lifted a hand in silent acknowledgment and disappeared down the corridor. She threw down the quilt and, grabbing a long T-shirt from her bureau drawer, yanked it over her head.

"You look cute," commented Ted. "But where the hell are you going?"

"It must be Andrew. I'll just get rid of him."

But when she got to the front door, she saw it wasn't Andrew. It was Paul. His deep-set eyes looked even deeper than usual. His mouth was a thin line. In the yellowish light from the nearby street lamp, his face seemed drained of all natural color.

"We've got to talk," he croaked. It was only from his voice that she could tell he'd been crying.

"You're drunk," she said.

"So are you."

That was fair. She started to step outside.

"No, inside."

"But I—"

"Make him leave."

Without another word spoken, she left Paul by the door and went back to the bedroom. Ted lay diagonally across the sheets, idly fingering his penis. He smiled at the sight of her, then frowned.

"What's wrong?"

"You'll have to go."

"Why? Is it an emergency?"

"No, it's Paul. He wants to talk to me."

At this Ted's face expressed disbelief. "'He wants to talk to me,'" he mimicked her voice, making it higher and sappier than it was. "What kind of game are you playing here? Did you plan this all out, just to make the old boyfriend jealous?"

"Don't be ridiculous," she snapped. "How could I have planned it? You're the one that came after *me*." But even as she spoke she could feel herself blushing. Something about his accusation sounded the truth, however distantly.

"You weren't exactly hard to get."

"Get out." She stood by the door, her arms crossed over her chest. "You, of all people, have no right to pull the moral high ground on me, with what's-her-name—"

"Cheryl."

"With Cheryl waiting dutifully at home."

"Oh, the old they-that-live-by-the-sword line, eh?"

"Whatever. Just get dressed and get out."

Which he did, more speedily than she could have imagined possible. He must be awfully practiced at these quick getaways, she thought. She followed him down the hallway and saw him give a silent mock-salute to Paul, who merely turned toward the wall with a frown. When Paul looked back at her, she beckoned him into the bedroom.

"So what's the story?" she said, plopping herself onto the wildly disordered bed.

Paul took the chair by the door. The room was so small that this placed him only five feet away from her. "*You* know."

"But I want to hear you say it."

"All right. You win. I'm jealous. Are you satisfied?"

"You act like I did it just to make you jealous."

"Didn't you?"

"No." He gave her a sharp, disbelieving glance. "At least, not consciously. He got to me in a weak moment, and I found him persuasive."

"But you've always hated Ted!"

"Well, maybe I was wrong about him. Or maybe you can be attracted to someone you hate. I never noticed that *you* were so perfect at keeping your feelings straight."

He closed his eyes and leaned his head back against the wall. She took this as a concession, or enough of one.

"Anyway, I thought we were through, you and I. History. Water under the bridge. No more obligations on either side, and no more feelings for each other."

He opened his eyes. "Do you really believe that?"

"I thought I did." She swallowed, feeling suddenly a little sick again. "And, more to the point, I thought you did."

He nodded. "I thought so too. But when I saw you go off with Ted—Jesus!" He clenched his fists, then noticed and relaxed them. "Anyway, it made me realize that I couldn't let things go the way they were. I mean, I know everything is over between us and I know you're going back to America next week. And I might never see you again. So I thought—I realized—" He stopped for a moment and cleared his throat, then spoke in such a low voice she could hardly hear him. "I couldn't let you go without telling you how much I loved you."

She was silent with shock. Then, "You never said."

"I know. I didn't want to give you that power over me. And then, tonight, I realized I hadn't saved myself by not telling you. I'd given you that power anyway. So I thought you might as well know. No—I didn't *think* anything, in a rational way. I just had to tell you."

"I'm glad." She smiled at him, and he smiled back. "I love you too."

"I know."

"You know! You always were an arrogant bastard."

He laughed. "No, it's not that. It was the green scarf. When I lost it in the dining room, I was really upset. I looked everywhere for it, but I never found it. I decided someone must have stolen it. And then, this Easter, when you made that little pile of stuff I'd given you and put it by my door—that's when I realized. I realized *you'd* taken the scarf. Right?"

"Yes. Yes, I did."

"And I was supposed to guess that, and come get it back. Right?"

"I don't know. Maybe."

"Well, I'm here now. Can I have it?"

She got up from the bed and went to the bureau, where she knelt and opened the bottom drawer. From under her sweaters she drew the green mohair scarf. He reached out and she gave it to him. Then she sat back down on the bed.

"Thank you." They were quiet a moment, looking at each other. Just then there was a loud knock on the door. She heard Andrew's voice calling her.

"Are you all right? Please, just open the door so I can check on you. I came by and the front door of the hostel was wide open, so I got worried. . . . Hello? Are you there?"

She rolled her eyes at Paul in an "Oh, Christ!" manner. He pointed at the closet door, then silently got up, opened the closet, and closed himself inside. "I'll be right there," she yelled.

As she got out of bed for the third time that evening, it occurred to her that her life was beginning to resemble the French farce she had seen the previous week in the West End.

Then another wave of nausea roiled up in her. Tomorrow would be a hangover day, she was sure. Had she ever been this drunk before? Hard to know. She was too drunk to compare.

She opened her bedroom door onto Andrew's worried face.

"Oh, thank heavens, you're all right. I just got some kind of premonition and had to check on you. How are you feeling?"

She leaned forward, opened her mouth, and was sick all over his shoes.

When she had finished vomiting, she apologized profusely. Andrew apologized even more profusely for disturbing her. In a comedy of self-abnegation, he backed down the hallway, keeping up a litany of consolation and concern. "I should never have come by so late . . . I'll check on you tomorrow . . . No, no problem at all, they're easily cleaned . . . Just rest up and get better . . . I do hope it's not a relapse . . ."

She closed the bedroom door and opened the closet. Paul was scrunched on the floor, his head buried in his arms, his back shaking silently.

"Are you all right?" she asked, touching his shoulder tenderly.

He looked up at her and howled with laughter. Clutching his sides, he rolled out onto the floor of the room, still howling. It was contagious, and she began to giggle. Soon she was laughing so hard that tears came.

"Don't! It's mean!" she gasped.

"So it is. But it's hilarious. Anyway, I kind of enjoy being mean once in a while."

"I do too, but I've had enough of it tonight." She wiped her eyes. "I need to go rinse my face and brush my teeth. I can still taste the vomit."

"A pretty thought."

"Oh, shut up. I'll be right back."

When she returned, he was lying on the unmade bed. He patted the spot beside him and she lay down as well. They both stared at the ceiling.

"Will you analyze a dream for me?" he asked.

"Sure. When did you have it?"

"Right after we broke up, and just about every week since then. I had it again last night."

"Go ahead."

"I'm on a road," he began, "somewhere in England, I think, but nowhere I recognize. I'm walking, and it's night. And I have a strange feeling that something's going to happen. It's not fear exactly—more like anticipation. Then suddenly I'm in the midst of a blinding fog, and that's when I get frightened."

"What are you afraid of?" she asked.

He paused and considered. "That I'll never get out of the fog," he said.

"So what did the dream mean?" asked Adam as they sat, two days later, over their final cheese scones and morning coffee. The next day he would fly back to America; she was scheduled to go early the following week.

"Oh, you know—that he loved me and was afraid to admit it, because he would somehow lose all sense of his own direction if he attached that much importance to another person."

"Well, *that* didn't take any analysis. He'd already told you as much."

"*I* know that. And *you* know that. But these English people—"

They laughed.

"So are you and he back together?"

"No. We just had that one night, and that was it. Maybe we'll have another sometime—next year, or twenty years from now. But the relationship as it was is over." She sighed. "Have you ever noticed how you get everything you want in life, but only after you don't want it any more?"

"No, I haven't noticed that precise thing. Maybe my pattern is different."

"Maybe." She looked at him questioningly, but he deflected the question.

"And do you think Ted was telling the truth? Does he really visit Harold every week?"

"Who knows?" she shrugged. "He's such a practiced liar, he probably doesn't even know himself. What do you think the deep, dark secret was?"

"I wouldn't care to venture an opinion," Adam answered.

"You know, jealousy is a funny thing," she went on, as if changing tack. "I was thinking about it this morning. When you love someone, it's as if you give them a part of yourself. And if they sleep with someone else, it's like they're giving away that part of you to the other person. You feel it as that—

an actual possession that you treasure, being handed to someone else. Shakespeare understood that. That's what he was
talking about in *Othello*."

"The handkerchief."

"Yes. Exactly." She beamed at him. "It's so satisfying talking to someone who always knows what you mean. Are you
like this with everyone?"

"Only my friends."

They were silent for a short time. "Would you rather have
your own friends that you have now," she asked, "or friends
like the great writers who lived in England at the turn of the
century?"

"A ridiculous question."

"Why?"

"Because if I had those people as friends then I would be
one of them too, and not myself, so of course I would prefer
them to my present friends. But since I don't, I'm not, and so
I can't."

"Can't? You only prefer me to Henry James because you
can't have him?"

"You're twisting my words again."

"I always do."

"Yes. An inveterate tendency toward fictionalizing. Perhaps you'll turn out to be a great turn-of-the-century writer
after all," he teased her.

She waved aside his irony. "With my luck, I'll probably
turn out to be one of the subordinate scribblers."

"You should be so lucky."

"What, you don't think I'm good enough?"

"I haven't a clue. All I know is that you haven't written anything yet."

"Well, neither have you."

"Yes, but I'm not announcing my hubris to the world."

He smiled to soften it, and she smiled back. "You're not exactly the world."

At this he sighed. "Too true. I had forgotten."

After he left her, she wandered back to the long, light room where the reference works and bound periodicals were kept. But instead of choosing something to read, she put her head down on the table to think, and soon fell into a light sleep.

She dreamed she was walking in a large, high-walled garden. By her side was Adam. He knew all about the trees and plants, and was telling her about each one. Then they came out into a large open space, and in front of them was a strange tower, a kind of transplanted Chinese pagoda, with tier upon tier extending upward. It looked very familiar to her, as if she had seen it in a dream. They stopped in front of it.

"It's so—complete," said Adam.

"Yes," she said.

He tucked her hand into the crook of his arm and they walked around the tower together, observing it from all sides, carefully and attentively, as if this close scrutiny would eventually yield them some kind of answer.